SHORELINES 2010
SHORT FICTION AND POETRY
FROM BRIGHTON'S NIGHTWRITERS

Published in Great Britain 2009 by Brighton Nightwriters

ISBN 0-9544299-8-2
9780954429980

Printed by Lightning Source

Brighton Nightwriters have been getting together once a week to discuss each others' work in a friendly, supportive atmosphere for over ten years. Some of us have been with going along since the beginning, some are complete newcomers; some attend regularly, some irregularly.

Brighton Nightwriters meets upstairs at *The Pub with No Name* at the top of Southover Street every Wednesday at 7.30pm.

New writers are always welcome - just come along or contact Tim Shelton-Jones on (01273) 505642 for more information.

www.nightwriters.org.uk

CONTENTS

DENNIS HICKSON The Road to Paradise　　4
LORNA KENT Poems　　12
COLIN CHALMERS Where now then?　　16
　　Right I just want to say…　　20
SIMON DAVIS Poems　　23
SEAN CAMPBELL Rhubarb and Custard　　26
ADRIAN CAINES Thank you　　31
JONATHAN CHAMBERLAIN The Boat　　32
MOSS RICH Poems　　36
ALASDAIR CRAIG Sky's the limit　　38
SIAN EVANS Poems　　42
ROB PARAMAN *From* Having the Glide　　46
ENZO MARRA Poems　　58
LIZ JALLA The Blind Date　　62
TIM SHELTON-JONES Poems　　69
NOREEN BROWN *From* Shadows Before　　75
ALANNA MCINTYRE Poems　　80
TANYA MURRAY Lamia, dressed in all of Mary　　86
　　Undying　　92
JAY ELSE Epiphany　　98
OLIVER ANDREW Poems　　102
NATALIE CURTIS Daddy　　108
　　Acceptance　　109
　　Summer Holiday　　110
THE NIGHTWRITERS　　112

DENNIS HICKSON

The Road to Paradise

Shamell awoke to the sound of his father dragging bags of grain to the front of the shop where he piled them on top of one another. A lone candle twisted and danced to every movement as the light jumped around the room bringing with it the excited swirls of dust. His mother was sitting up clutching her baby to her breast, her anxious face firmly fixed on her husband.

Shamell was just five years old, yet he knew this was no ordinary night. He heard the voices. At first they were nothing more than muffled shouts from afar accompanied by a distant tinkling of glass. It then crept nearer and the audible sound of the mob was accompanied by terrifying screams. His father's usually wise and considerate face had now adopted a demonic appearance in the candle light; contorted, twisted with bulging tearful eyes, which made him look like a crazed stranger who knew nothing of this world. He looked back and forth from his wife to his son, almost pleading forgiveness for his predicament as the protector, the father, the patriarch that could no longer protect.

Abdul was a good man, a religious man, well known at the Rama Sipri Mosque, in Ahmedabad. The small shop they ran on Vivekanand road, that sold rice and spices, was by no means a lucrative business, but it was sufficient to support the family. It would be a common sight to see Abdul, outside the shop, laughing and joking with customers and passers by.

Abdul had many Hindu friends as well as Muslim, and felt no less of one or the other. He was adamant that killing innocent Hindus was not the way forward and stressed the need for the two communities to live in peace side by

4

side. Ahmedabad was a dusty old city and Vivekanand road was a hot spot of activity, with trucks - which seemed to be in competition - with a wide assortment of colourful lights, flowers, and various pictures of gods in their cabs, going past at regular intervals belching out clouds of thick black diesel fumes that seemed to linger and coat everything in their path.

Abdul's mother, a huge woman with very few teeth, would say the reason that ethnic tension was so high in the city, was due to everyone waiting for the dust to settle, and in Ahmedabad, that was just not going to happen. Abdul's wife Amina would sometimes sit in the back room with her mother-in-law drinking tea and giggling. 'That is not how a wife is meant to behave,' he would say, only for his mother to rise up and mimic him, wagging her finger as she did so, which would make them laugh even more. Abdul would try to hide his smile as he left the room shaking his head.

Shamell loved his grandmother, who would bounce him on her knee and show him off to all her female friends… 'This is my grandson,' she would proudly exclaim to any stranger that ventured into the shop. They would often have their afternoon nap together as her huge plump figure would act as the most comfortable of cushions. It would please Amina to see them both asleep like a bear and her cub, she thought the world of her mother-in-law and would really look forward to their time together. She made her laugh with her strange anecdotes, many of which were about Amina's husband when he was a child. If he ever heard them he would laugh along also or look up as if he was asking Allah…what am I going to do with her?

On Fridays he would shut the shop and take Shamell to the local mosque, the women would go also and help prepare the food. He would usually meet his brother Assim who would have his three boys with him. The youngest of these was Muhammad aged nine, followed by Igbol, twelve, and Ali, thirteen. They would tease Shamell, especially Muhammad, who would pinch him when no one was looking and then dart off somewhere out of sight.

It was only a short walk to the mosque down the dusty main road, where the trucks would weave their way past the ox drawn carts, rickshaws, thousands of bicycles and the multitude of cows. Monkeys would sit by the side of the road in pairs as if they were bemused by the whole human race. Inside the mosque was a sort of refuge from all this, as it was immaculately clean and the outside world was silenced. Only the prayers could be heard in the mosque, but even with the help of outside speakers they were, beyond the mosque, drowned out by the continuous drone of traffic. Abdul would always leave the mosque feeling in a state of belonging, the whole week's problems would be washed away.

His father, before he died two years previously, had attended the same mosque, and he had hoped, one day, Shamell would also take his sons there. It was not always harmonious though, especially during election time, when there were often groups of BJP members standing on corners with microphones, which only needed a spark to ignite a bloody riot.

In 1992, militant Hindus demolished the 16th century Babri Mosque in Ayodhya, Uttar Pradesh, Northern India. These hard liners felt justified in doing so as they believed the mosque sat on the birthplace of Lord Rama, one of the most revered deities in Hinduism. They vowed to build a Hindu temple on the same spot stating it had been a holy pilgrimage site for centuries. What followed was the worst nation-wide rioting between Hindus and Muslims since Independence in 1947. The spark was well and truly lit. There had already been Hindu killings by Muslims in revenge for the destruction of the Babri Mosque and it was inevitable that Muslim deaths would follow.

The smashing of wood and the agonising cries of pain were now just a few shops away. Abdul gathered his family, took them to the back of the shop and began loading them in the cellar, which was nothing more than a small store cupboard. Amina was clinging on to his sleeves, sobbing, knowing there was no room for him as well. Even as it was, the flap did not shut down properly as there was precious little time to empty it. Abdul pulled his wife's arm away without being conscious of doing so, as all the time he had his eyes firmly fixed on the front of the shop.

Then the first crash, followed by a frenzied attack on the shutters which gave way like balsa wood under the violent onslaught of the crowd. As the bags of grain toppled, the first burning torch landed in the shop. Abdul picked it up in a vain attempt to save his life, furiously swinging it around to put off his tormentors. The first rock knocked him backwards and as he did so Shamell, through the gap in the cellar flap, saw his father's terrified face as the first hatchet sliced his head: a synchronic moment in time that slammed into Shamell's unconscious.

They were on him like a pack of wolves, every blow bouncing the torso like a fish in shallow water, soaking his white muslin suit in blood. Shamell could see their demented hate filled faces, bubbling over with the thrill of the kill, as the shop became the next victim; everything was pulled from the shelves and smashed, before being set ablaze. Smoke quickly filled the room as a burning cupboard landed on the cellar flap, trapping its occupants.

The frenzied mob departed like a violent vacuum leaving only devastation behind. Smoke was now pouring into the cellar. Shamell tried to squeeze out of the gap under the cupboard, he was coughing uncontrollably as his lungs filled with smoke, his mother was forcing his little body through the diminutive gap. The rage of the fire filled his ears as he pulled himself clear of the cupboard, heaving violently, unable to see through the choking smoke. He headed for where he felt was the front of the shop, the heat on his back was unbearable. Shamell stumbled outside into the street with his clothes ablaze and felt a hand grab his arm, then he passed out.

Ahmedabad the next day resembled a war zone. Two hundred and thirty six people lost their lives, including seven from Shamell's family, as Assim's shop was on the same street and one of the first to be attacked. Only Ali and their grandmother survived, although their shops did not. It was over two months before Shamell was walking again, due to the effects of smoke inhalation and the burns he suffered to his back, legs and arms. Except for the small income their grandmother made from selling flowers, Ali became the main breadwinner by shining shoes at Ahmedabad railway station and selling fruit from a mobile stall.

This family was a totally different entity from the one left behind. The grandmother was no longer the happy go lucky toothless smiling woman who made everyone laugh. She was now just a shell; an epitaph of her former self. Her multitude of expressions and anecdotes were now replaced by a monotone voice and a blank stare that induced sorrow into whomever she looked upon. Her idiosyncratic behaviour had simply been reduced to automatism. Within a year she was dead.

If there was one positive thing to be dragged from that pernicious night of madness, it was the metamorphosis of Ali. He took to his new adult role in an assiduous manner, which even the death of his grandmother, which resulted in them being forced out of their one room to live on the streets, did not sway him from his task. By the time Shamell was ten, Ali had given him direct control of the shoe shine 'business,' while he worked on the stall. They were for a long time sleeping on the railway station platform with the multitude of the ragged destitute.

These were the untouchables, the lowest cast, the people Mahatma Gandhi renamed the 'Harijans', the children of God. Although this was meant to be a Hindu peculiarity, anyone, whether Hindu or Muslim who found themselves in the same predicament would be issued with the same derogatory title. Ali's positive outlook eventually had a profound effect on Shamell who had seemed to have inherited his late grandmother's sense of humour.

One day Shamell was in his usual place outside the railway station when he was approached by a big fat man who ran a brothel nearby. It was quite unusual to see someone that huge in Ahmedabad and this man looked angry. He walked over to Shamell and kicked his shoeshine box down the steps spilling all the contents, he then grabbed him by his shirt, ripping it in the process, and threw him to the floor shouting obscenities about how he was ruining his business.

As always, in Ahmedabad, when an incident of this sort happened, a crowd began to gather and just at that point Ali arrived on the scene. Ali ran straight up to the fat man from behind and threw a huge cloth over his head while still keeping hold of it. The man, not being able to see, was swinging his arms around furiously trying to rid himself of the cloth. The crowd by this point were hysterical, especially when he lost his balance and fell flat on his backside on the top step with the cloth still attached to his face, with Ali screaming 'Leave my cousin alone you fat bastard!' which sent the crowd into raptures of laughter.

While the man desperately tried to pull off the cloth, Shamell, who had a gangly appearance - he was all legs and arms-took up the pose of a boxer and continuously jabbed him in the face. He toppled backwards and slid down the stairs on his bottom, to the sheer ecstatic jubilation of the crowd, which was growing by the minute. Ali gestured to Shamell to pick up his shoe shining box and they both headed off through the crowd just as the fat man managed to wrestle off the cloth.

He was furious, and began attacking people who were standing in the crowd, only to be seen by passing police in a land rover, who immediately jumped out, were also attacked, drew their batons, overpowered him and bundled him into the back of their vehicle. The boys, in seeing the police vehicle pull up, wandered back to watch the show. Ali looked at Shamell, they were both quite shaken, and asked him if he was alright. Shamell replied... 'Alright!...of course I'm alright, I've got the fat bastard's watch.' With that Shamell pulled a gold watch out of his pocket..

Ali was astounded, he screamed with laughter, throwing his arms around his cousin who was beaming, from ear to ear. 'We are going to go far, cousin,' Ali laughed. There was one person in the crowd though, a man in a clean, smart muslin suit, who did not join in with the laughter, but watched the event unfold with dedicatory curiosity. He only allowed himself a sly smile and then walked away.

The incident with the fat man was to end up being the worst mistake the boys ever made, and one month later it all came to a head. Ali had just put his mobile stall back in its usual place, tucked up around the back of the market, and was going off to the station to meet Shamell. As he turned up a dark cobbled street, he noticed two figures blocking his way.

'Where's my watch... Muslim?' snarled the fat man. Ali immediately raised his arms in the air and declared his innocence... 'Watch?...I know nothing of any watch... you must be mistaken,' He tried to weave round them. 'No, Muslim...you made the mistake,' the fat man said as he grabbed Ali by the throat.

Two hours later, Shamell was waiting in the usual spot for his cousin to arrive; it was not like him to be late, as they usually went together to find something to eat. Shamell decided to walk to where Ali put his stall. The sight that met his eyes as he turned down the cobbled street rivaled the memories of his father's death when he was in that cramped cellar. He could scarcely believe the crumpled bloody mess that was lying on the floor was his cousin. Ali was everything to him, he was his father; his brother; his cousin, and most of all, his best friend. Ali was part of him, they were one and the same. There was nothing without him, no reason to live.

Shamell grabbed hold of his cousin's broken body, then with all his strength, dragged him into the street screaming for someone to help him. At first he was met by the usual ominous stares of the public, but then a smartly dressed Muslim man marched over and took hold of Ali's blood stained body.

'I'm sorry Shamell,' he said after a while, 'your cousin is dead.' Shamell, not even registering that the man knew his name, began to scream at the top of his voice... 'Noooo!....he can't be,' as he began shaking his cousin's corpse, sobbing uncontrollably... 'Don't leave me...Ali!...don't fucking leave me... please.' He collapsed onto his cousin's body, crying, muttering, sobbing. He remained in that position, with the Muslim man at his side, until the ambulance came with police in tow. The police took statements, from people in the crowd and the Muslim man; but as for Shamell all he would say was ... 'It was that fat bastard,'... at which point the police gave each other strange looks and stated that there would be a thorough investigation.

The lifeless body of Ali was loaded into the ambulance to be taken straight to the mortuary. Shamell was still trying to hang on to his cousin and it was the Muslim man who pulled him gently away, and held him by both arms and said... 'You will have to be strong Shamell...the time has come for you to fight... I will take great pleasure in taking revenge for this outrage...this fat man who runs his house of filth, will no longer hurt another Muslim, that is a promise I make to you ...but first of all you must come with me, I have a place you may stay.' Shamell was still sobbing, soaked in his cousin's blood, yet the man's words wormed their way into his unconscious.

There is Ali he thought, I can see him, and he's alive, pushing his barrow down the street. 'Ali!' Shamell screamed as he ran towards his cousin, 'Ali...it's me...wait,' but he just kept on walking. Shamell ran up to him and put his hand on his shoulder... 'Ali...where are you going,' he exclaimed. When Ali turned around, his face was bloody and caved in. He said in a slow demonic voice... 'I'm going to hell.' Shamell then noticed his father on the barrow, with half of his face missing, trying to mutter in the same tone... 'Shamell...Shamell...Shamell'.... 'Shamell wake up,' said a voice as he leapt into consciousness with a start.

The smart man who had found him yesterday was standing over him. His name was Muhammad Khan. 'It is time to avenge your cousin's death,' he said. He took Shamell into an adjacent room where there was a group of men waiting. They all looked very pleased to see him. One man, Hussein Bin Mullah, presented Shamell with two new suits. They all expressed their deepest sympathies regarding what had happened to Shamell and they relayed to Shamell how much they had admired his and Ali's father, as they were good Muslims from good Muslim families and it was an outrage that they met their deaths the way they did; killed by Hindus. They told Shamell that they had already arranged for Ali to have a decent Muslim funeral; everything had been taken care of. There would be prayers in the Rama Sipri Mosque tomorrow. At that point, Shamell awoke from his trance-like state.

'I cannot go there,' he protested, 'that's where I used to go with my father.'

'Do not turn your back on your family, Shamell,' Hussein said gently. 'It is time to stop running away...it is time to respect who you are, in the good name of your father, it is time to fight....tonight will be the first in a glorious fight to win back your family's honour.'

Shamell stood for a moment thinking, for he had never actually thought about who killed his parents or why? He had just smothered those painful thoughts and had kept them hidden, but the more he thought about it now, the more he believed these people to be right. He grew angry when he thought of Ali. 'I will go to the mosque,' he exclaimed, 'and tonight I will gladly help avenge the death of my dearest cousin.' It shocked him as he said it and what startled him even more was the small smile which crept into the corner of his mouth.

'Welcome,' Hussein said... 'from now on you are our brother.' They all shook his hand and greeted him like a new family member.

Once outside, Muhammad and Shamell were stalking the narrow dark streets, moving quickly and avoiding any areas where there may be groups of people. It was 3am and the only creatures present were the city's scurrying rats and the crumpled up homeless hidden in doorways.

Muhammad had told Shamell that the reason the fat man had got out of prison and would not be investigated by the police for his cousin's death was due to the local Chief of Police being a regular visitor of his filthy establishment and more than willing to take bribes. The fat man, as usual, was waiting outside his door in the dimly lit back street. The only noise was an overflow pipe which gushed out onto the cobbled street two doors down.

He was smoking a cigarette waiting to lure in his next customer. Shamell shouted...'You fat bastard, you killed my cousin!' and with that the fat man chased Shamell around the corner. Out of a doorway stepped Muhammad with a raised pistol and shot him square in the forehead. Muhammad calmly walked over and pumped three more bullets into his torso. Shamell had never felt so powerful and satisfied. 'Now we've killed you... you fat bastard,' Shamell said, before spitting on the body and quickly walking away.

The next day Shamell went to pay his respects to Ali at the Rama Sipri Mosque. After prayers, Shamell sat down with Muhammad, Hussein, Aziz, Omah and Mahmud. They discussed the plight of Muslims in the world and told Shamell he was not alone, as Muslims had lost their lives and families in all corners of the globe; in Chechnya, Palestine, Iraq, Afghanistan and Kashmir, to name but a few. Muslims from all over the world were now fighting back. After a while they instinctively sensed that Shamell would like to be left alone with his thoughts. In the peacefulness of the mosque, Shamell prayed and prayed and prayed.

He saw his father's jovial face, standing in his clean muslin suit with his mother beside him, holding his baby sister in her arms, lifting her to show him. Assim walked up with Muhammad and Igbol; Muhammad was making pinching gesture with his fingers and giggling. Then his toothless smiling grandmother stepped forward, with all her sparkle restored, how happy she looked. Last of all, there stood dearest Ali, his arms outstretched in a gesture that said...' It is up to you cousin.' Shamell knew from that moment why he was still alive. If he wanted to join his family in paradise he would have to achieve martyrdom.

Three years later in a Kashmir valley, a lorry turned around a bend and crunched into a higher gear. Shamell could hear the chants of Muslim prayers, defiantly reverberating around the Himalayas, as he sped down the mountain towards the army barracks. He could hear the shouts of soldiers as he passed them, firing their guns. Shamell was laughing out loud, tears of joy were running down his face, he could see his family waving, smiling, waiting, as the last flimsy barrier gave way on his final road to paradise.

LORNA KENT

The Butterfly Dress

The oxygen cylinder
had been gone for a month.
I moved the rug to hide the impression
but I still could not sit in your chair.

A tower of newspapers slumped
against the wall, unread.
The bread turned green, then black
and I thought it would never
stop raining.

For months my head ached
to the sound of you
sucking the last of life from the air.
The silence was worse;
that day you stopped treading water
and I watched you slowly sink
below the surface.

They got someone to phone me you know;
tried to coax me out
with kind and gentle words.
She was persistent, I'll give her that.
Finally, I agreed to meet her at the station.
"I'll be wearing my butterfly dress," she said.
And I felt the forgotten warmth
of a smile flush across my face.

The Palmist

Slow anemone fingers
suck him into her amniotic dark.

Drugged by her paraffin warmth
he offers his palm,
belly up like a turtle stranded
on the beach.

Her fingers ride
this stranger's muscled flesh,
teasing cryptic strands
from a living map of dead ends.
Like a lover she whispers
only what he wants to hear.

So many years spent casting for futures
on the end of this burnt-match pier.
She breathes with the swell and dip of the sea;
the faint smell of gin on her breath.

Even as the money hits the tin
he's starting to forget.
She takes another nip from the bottle
and releases him
squinting into the light.

All Night Cafe

A shock of white light
shrinks your pupils to full stops.
Two fluorescent strips
incubate a strange brood;
dishevelled survivors of the night.
A blue haze hangs in the air
and the smell of bacon
promises more than it can deliver.

By the cigarette machine
a businessman checks his breath;
waits for the girl with ivory thighs
who looked old enough in the club.
She's in a spin
throwing up his double vodkas
in a loo with no lock, no light
and no back way out.

A shrunken hag with a map for a face
keeps her hair in a wig
and her life in a bag.
She's forgotten where she's going,
can't remember where she's been;
eats fried eggs with a spoon
and spits out imaginary ants;
one last rotten tooth defying the world.

Two teenage boys share acne
and a sense of immortality,
hide a can of Special Brew under the table
and try to bum a smoke.
A fumble or a fight, it makes no odds
as long as someone's face
hits the pillow or the pavement.

A pair of sisters, thin as whippets
hard-face each other over a tin ashtray,
suck on roll-ups with a vengeance
and listen to the jukebox
telling tales of drunkenness and cruelty.
Still waiting for that sunny afternoon,
their inevitable lives tug
at the corners of their mouths.

A long-distance lorry driver
elbows the mist from the window,
watches the rain in the headlights
of a waiting taxi
and thinks of his soft pink wife
in their duck-down duvet;
the TV flickering
in the dark.

Out the back,
a man with a grudge
and a carbon steel knife
spreads cut-price marg
on thick sliced white;
hums an unrecognisable tune
as the ash on his fag gets
dangerously long.

COLIN CHALMERS

Where now then?

"Where now then?" asked Pete, looking at Richard who was finishing off his drink then down at Christine who was still sitting at the table, texting. Neither replied.

"Flanagans?" Pete always wanted to go to Flanagans on Fridays, he had this crazy idea that one of the barmaids fancied him, based entirely on the fact that she had once put a smile on a pint of Guinness he'd ordered and winked at him.

"Fancy your chances then Pete?" said Christine without looking up from her texting, then murmured "Pathetic."

"I heard that," Pete said back, quick as a flash, "and you are so totally wrong, I won't say pathetic cause that would be rude, and I'm not rude, but you don't understand women and I do and I can tell you that wink was not customer courtesy it was..."

"What you talking about, I am a woman!"

"Yeah I know, but not really, not like, you know what I mean, you're just Christine."

"Cheers."

"Will you two stop it," says Richard, "and can we please decide where we're going?"

Christine put her phone away and stood up. "Anne-Marie's down the Hope, she's had a bit of a hard time today and I've said I'm going to meet her there, but if you want to go off somewhere else that's fine by me..."

"No" says Richard, "Hope, good idea, they're open till at least one, good enough for you Pete?"

Christine had her coat on by now and gestured to Pete to finish up, "Unless you're really desperate to see the girl who gave you the wank."

"Wink, it was a wink and it was a come on wink, jeez, you two know nothing."

"Wink, wank, whatever. Let's go," said Christine heading for the door, the other two following her, as they usually did, out into the street trying to keep up.

"Right," said Richard as they fell in with Christine's stride for the five minutes to the Hope, "like I was saying, they're not telling us the truth about this credit crunch, it's the oil, they know it's running out, all of them do, the people who run the bankers and the politicians and the people behind them and they're trying to slow down how much we use so they can sort nuclear fission before the Chinese do, who are worried about the the snow on the Himalayas, twelve feet a year that's going back by, which means no crops for them, which is why they want to move into Afghanistan, which is why we're there really of course, although..."

"Sure Richard," said Christine, "Great you've found all this out, and it's only you found it out, that's particularly impressive, maybe you should tell Anne-Marie that's why she's lost her job."

"Do no harm for her to know."

"She's what?" said Pete, "Lost that job at the library, because of the Chinese? That's a shame, she really liked that didn't she? You think she's needing a bit of comforting?"

"Don't even think it Pete," said Christine, "and none of your conspiracy bollocks either Richard, she really is quite upset. Look, when we get there you two go upstairs for a bit to the lounge bar so I can have a chat with her first, then you can come down and be friendly and understanding, not lechy and weird mind, ok?"

Pete and Richard, trying to keep up with Christine's formidable pace, reluctantly agreed and they were at the Hope before they knew it. As soon as they were in, Christine pointed to the stairs and Pete put his hands up in submission to her will, grabbing Richard who was heading into the main bar, and pulling him along.

"Ages since I've been up here," said Richard, looking around what was generally considered to be the more sophisticated part of the Hope, quieter, full of couples who looked like they were on a rare night out from the kids rather than the mix of students on the pull and wannabe DJs downstairs.

"Bit creepy innit?" said Pete, "But don't worry, we're only staying for one so Christine can do her what-a-shame-never-mind thing with Anne-Marie before we cheer her up. I've always liked Anne-Marie, very quiet right enough, perfect for being a librarian I suppose, though in my experience that can often mean a bit of a screamer, you know? There was one girl I knew..."

"Pete!" Richard whispered, moving alongside Pete at the bar, "Don't look now but your wank girl is right behind me. See her?"

"Wink, it was a wink for fuck sake. Where is she?" Pete moved to Richard's side to scan the tables behind him, and sure enough the barmaid from Flanagans was at the corner table, nursing a short and talking to an older bloke in a suit.

"You're right," Pete said, eyes lighting up, "It is her, dressed to kill as well." She was wearing a bright blue dress, short, allowing Pete to check out her legs, something he had singularly failed to do on any of their previous meetings despite one attempt which ended up with a barman accusing him of trying to steal the crisps behind the bar.

"She's on a date, isn't she?" said Richard, "Probably a bit out your league anyway. Listen before we go downstairs can I just emphasise that if you've got any money in a bank at the moment…"

Pete stared over at the barmaid and the bloke, assessing the situation. "That's no date, the body language's a dead give way, he's probably her boss or her dad or something. I'm going over."

"You can't do that!" whispered Richard as loudly as he could. "She's with a bloke in the upstairs bar, that's a date, you don't even know here name. You can't just…"

But Pete was already on his way, excusing himself through the groups of people standing between the bar and the table he was heading for, the epitomy of politiness and consideration for others.

"Thank you so much, just trying to get past, excuse me." He got to the table and stood almost against it, waiting for a few seconds until the couple noticed he was there and looked up.

"Can I help you?" said the bloke.

"Na, you're alright, just wanted to say hello again to your companion."

"Oh you're a friend of Sadie's?"

"That's right, eh Sadie?" Pete said and winked at her.

"I'm sorry, who are you?" said Sadie looking up at Pete with a polite smile then over at the bloke, then back.

"You remember," said Pete, winking at her again "you gave me a wank in Flanagans." Pete realised he hadn't said exactly what he'd intended to but thought this was recoverable, maybe even quite endearing, something they'd look back at together and laugh about uproariously.

The bloke looked like he was in a state of shock. "Sorry, are you saying Sadie…"

"No, no, sorry, I'm afraid I'm a bit pissed, shouldn't really have said that."

Pete turned to the girl who, now they were getting better aquainted, he knew to be called Sadie. "Don't mean to offend you or your dad or whoever you are, just saying hello really, nice to see you outside your work setting, and I must say you look delightful."

"This is my date, who the fuck are you?"

The bloke turned to Sadie, "You gave him a wank and you don't even remember him? This is weird, last time I'm going on Guardian soulmates I tell you, sorry Sadie, all a bit wild side for me, I'm off."

"Nigel, I don't even know him…"

"And I'm sure that's just how you like your fuck buddies or whatever you call them, all anonymous and no strings, it's just not my scene ok?"

As the bloke stood up Sadie leaned over to him trying to grab his jacket, but the bloke pulled himself free. With Sadie concentrating on getting hold of the bloke's jacket, Pete saw the perfect opportunity to try out this thing he'd read about on the internet the week before - The Game, a scientifically proven technique for pulling any female you fancy that basically involves touching them when they're thinking about something else so they won't know you've touched them but will be dead keen to shag you. He went for a gentle caress on the shoulder, but as he did this Sadie turned to him and his hand landed on her right breast, not exactly his intended move. However this was probably ok too, Pete thought, because according to The Game if you think of a distraction your move isn't noticed, it's just taken in subconsciously and the female you're after just fancies you rotten without knowing why.

"Did you know that library jobs are being cut in this borough because of the oil in the Himalayas?"

Before Sadie could answer, Richard grabbed Pete, pulling him away to the stairs.

"Sorry about that," Richard said to Sadie, who was covering her chest with her arms in what looked like a foetal position, her mouth open but with nothing coming out. "He's a bit mixed up, the oil's not in the Himalayas obviously, that would be ridiculous. But get your money out the bank."

They walked towards the stairs. "Where now then?" said Pete.

Right I just want to say...

"Right I just want to say I think it's great we're all here, we're all here for a purpose, I think we can all agree on that and I think we can also agree what that purpose is - getting what's best for our community, making the changed we all want to see. Now I'm sure there's going to be disagreements, and that's fine, that's part of what we're here for, but I'm sure that when issues arise where there are differences between us – I would say us stakeholders, but lets leave the jargon to one side today, yeah? – that when there are differences between us I hope we can see these differences as challenges we can meet, something we can work on together and make progress on, not blocks to the progress we all want, but opportunities to get to know each other, to get things moving, opportunities that let us celebrate our differences and move on together, really achieve something. Everyone ok with that?"

The coffee isn't really coffee I'm thinking, it's a sort of milky foam dished into plastic cups so fragile they struggle to stand up. Everyone seems to have one but no one's drinking it. Mostly folk seem to be looking about, anywhere but at Roger, my line-manager at the council and our introductory speaker for the morning, who keeps trying to catch people's eyes but just gets twitchy smiles and a look away instead.

"So who wants to start? As I say, this is all about being open with each other, whatever you want to say, that's fine." Like fuck it is I'm thinking, wondering whose going to be daft enough to speak first. There's thirteen of us; some council officials like me slumming it for the afternoon out here in 'the community' miles from latte land , a couple of older people I've never seen before who are whispering to each other and smiling at no one in particular, probably at the wrong meeting or not caring what meeting they're at, and of course a few 'community leaders', self-appointed obviously, people used to being told, and believing, that what they say counts when nearly everyone else knows that's bollocks, that the real decisions about this place get made in meetings in rooms a long way away from here. But not quite everyone. Not Sarah, the new Local Community Networks Coordinator, for instance I'm thinking as she coughs a bit, ready to break the silence.

"Thanks Roger, I think everyone's very happy with that, and I'd just like to say how much I think we all really value the chance to input into these plans, because these changes are going to mean a lot for our community - I think I can say our community as someone who works here - and it's great that the council is listening to what the community thinks rather than just doing things without consultation, I think that really means a lot to everyone."

I wonder if she believes this, or even knows what she's saying, but I reckon she's just in some sort of zone where she can talk without saying anything, come out with words that when she's finished and you try working out what she's said you realise she's said nothing at all.

Sarah hasn't finished. "Maybe it would be good if I started, would that be ok?"

Indifference is taken as consent. "Ok then, I'll just say three things – process, process, process. That's what matters here, that we all buy into this process and make it work. If we don't, this is all just a waste of time! So I'd certainly like to back up what Roger says about the importance of honesty in the whole process, because we all have our own experiences, we all have our areas of knowledge, I think we need to acknowledge that, acknowledge each other and what we bring here, value that, celebrate that we're all here, from all our different backgrounds, with all our different beliefs, and we're determined to work for a positive outcome, an outcome with real value, not just talking for the sake of it, but real, open honest discussions because it's not going to be much use to anyone us sitting here and discussing things if we aren't honest, is it?"

Sarah laughs. Maybe it's a joke. But no one else laughs. Everyone's got the resigned look of commuters waiting for a train that's late and there's nothing they can do about it. There's a bit of a silence, but it doesn't mean Sarah's finished. She just likes silences so she can fill them in.

"Ok, so lets take that as a starting point, yeah? Great. Will I kick off?" Silence. "Ok then, well I suppose, and I will be honest here, I suppose I think it's important to stress the need for real engagement with the changes we're talking about here, the need to really buy into them. I'm not saying we're there yet, there's going to be a lot of work to be done pulling this together, but I do think that if we can get to a place where we all agree something needs to be done we'll have got somewhere, made real progress. My experience of this sort of thing, and I don't mean to minimise the input of people who are new to this sort of collaboration because new blood is important, great to have Roger and the others on board, crucial really, but I suppose what I'm saying is I have a lot of experience of this sort of process and that experience tells me that if we pull together and don't get caught up in the sort of infighting that does no one any good, then we can make things really happen, not quickly, not overnight, but make real progress nonetheless. And let's remember, I think we all have to remember this, and I'm sure we all do, but it's probably worth saying anyway, let's remember that this isn't about us, this is about our community, the people with no voice here, the people who we represent. They're who really count. Lets remember that and lets take a leaf out of the great man of the moment and say" – she pauses for a reaction but there isn't any – "'Yes we can!' Because if we think that, don't just pretend to, but really think like that, really believe in ourselves and our abilities to change things, well, I really do think we really can."

It's 10 minutes in now and I'm thinking 80 more. Jesus. Roger's been looking at his watch for the last 5 minutes, a message Sarah is oblivious to, and seems keen to move on. "Thanks Sarah, really important that we lay that stuff out, put down ground rules, I thought I might have done that initially, but always good to have these things reinforced. I'm wondering if anyone else has anything to say, maybe someone wants to start moving onto the precise core of what we're here for, anyone, Joe?"

Jeez, right at me, what a bastard. Still can't do any harm if I just keep with the flow. "Thanks Roger, just taking in Sarah's points really at the moment, thanks Sarah, really useful as ever, and I suppose I'm really interested to hear other people's views too. Is that what everyone else thinks, that they'd like to hear other people's points of view?"

A few people nod, but Roger isn't letting me off that easy. "I'm sure we all would, great idea, maybe we should go round and get initial views from everyone, maybe start with you Joe. Thoughts?"

Everyone's looking at me, for a moment they look like lost children, wondering why they've been abandoned here and wanting rescued. But they aren't. They're just blank and waiting their turn. I'm the lost one, and I've no thoughts at all.

SIMON DAVIS

organism

in a jaundiced bed of win
what drugs how with obsessions of have

monochrome the rainbows
as indifferent whether takes a turn for the now

red exit stage right
blue exit stage left

a fervour of whichs blow overhead
wantonly spearing any from the barrel

cast out onto foreign sures
how-to-where this must covered duress

then why, the charnel house phoenix
bonds our questions to banish dolour

general sherman sees lindsey creek waiting[1]
and shudders at the candour of wildflowers

---

[1] General Sherman, the largest living tree on earth (by volume). Lindsey Creek, was its larger predecessor, uprooted in a storm (1905).

UNDER

UNDERSTANDING

STANDS

CHOICE.

GOD

CHOOSES

PRIEST

CHOOSES

child

CHOOSES

SADNESS

Simon Davis

In the begging inn

In the begging inn one was perfect in state of mind and body conshushiness
with pillows plump
till cashed out of the dark and ideas came riding tutus,
Billowing, ballet-ing and eventually balloting for three's a crowd
Demonstrating nothing better than Hoovers stashed into
Cubhoards of trained alstations
Dobermanned by fuckwit humour tumours
a'labottomized pit pony expression, less
There's a good kicking to be had (not shins) repeat…

Good kicking to behead the next man or
Manarchy in the you O.K?
I thought not, but listen
Do you want to know a secret?
Do you promise not to smell?
Because a perfumed ironed shirt is a steely gold charm guard
Until we learn how to dress out or more pert in antlers
Dress fancy, dress up like clown elegants in essence of attitude
With at least apportioned raison for starters…

Ready?
Contestants ready,
Steady and
Whoaaah! Betide ye rooted throng who still are still
Hunting witches only now the imagicnation lewds
into a lottery mysticism of numbers between
Hate, die, fear, and peddlewar randomly
Find the ladybird,
Find the gentlegeezer….

As round and round and round they go
Where they've gone nobody gives an escapology
Or even act-knowledges knocking you over or bumping
You off
Oh see you then
No never mind
No mind never
Not at all
Fall down with out a safety net or sign of a trap ease

Applications in rightwing to:
The Sir Cuss's
Hardly Fayre

SEAN CAMPBELL

Rhubarb and Custard

I loved those fish. Just two ordinary gold fish. I had a tank for them in my bedroom. Not one of those massive tropical ones and not one of those round bowls that look like an astronaut's helmet. Just a rectangular medium sized tank, about a metre in length with the Graf Spee sunk at the bottom.

That was a present I got from my aunt Kate. A model of the German Pocket Battleship the Admiral Graf Spee. It was great fun putting it together, following the step by step instructions, but what are you supposed to do with it then? I couldn't hang it from the ceiling with my World War II fighter collection, so I recreated what happened to it in real life and sunk it to the bottom of the fish tank. Rhubarb and Custard loved it, always swimming down to it and playing chase around it. Imagine what Admiral Donitz would have made of that. The pride of the German fleet scuttled at the bottom of a fish tank in my bedroom.

To be honest as much as I loved the fish they weren't my first choice of pet. I really wanted a dog but Mum refused to have one in the house. She said - the countryside is the only place for dogs, somewhere that they can run around. I suggested a rabbit but Dad was allergic to them. I went through the whole list. Hamsters, Mice, Gerbils. But the answer was no to all of them. It was - you'll never look after them - or - you'll forget to feed them - or - think of the poor little things locked up in their cage - or - you'll be so upset when they die and they will die you know, they never last long. So I kept asking, kept staring in pet shop windows when we were in town and eventually they caved in and dad bought me the two fish and a tank.

They had to be called Rhubarb and Custard, my favourite programme on TV. Mum kept nagging me that I was too old for cartoons but there was something about it that felt more real than what was going on around me. Mum was always saying I'd never get anywhere if I didn't stop being so childish, said I'd never get any friends. But she also kept saying that she never wanted to lay eyes on me hanging out with the likes of such and such. There was always something wrong with everyone my age that she encountered. That's why I never really left the house much. I didn't see the point really. I would just be aimlessly wandering the streets, bound to bump into one group of kids or another that at best would mean I would get shouted at and pushed about a bit. At worst I'd be beaten up again. The only times that I really went out was when we went shopping or I was dragged off fishing with dad.

I hated going fishing. I'm not even sure why he called it fishing. We'd just sit there in silence not catching a thing. I didn't mind that though. I couldn't help thinking about Rhubarb and Custard and how I would have hated to see them stuck on the end of a hook.

I don't know why he insisted that I went with him. I'd always moan and complain and he'd say that I wouldn't be making such a fuss if he took those two bloody fish down to the river and let them free to see if we could catch them again. It was always the same place we went to, down to the local river, down to the same bit of waste land on the outskirts of the town centre. There's a whole new block of luxury apartments there now. He could never be bothered to go any further, he just wanted to sit in the same place and stare at the water. Water that was full of old shopping trolleys, carrier bags and all the other rubbish that people had thrown away.

I remember one time there was this lad from the year above sat on the opposite bank from us. I can't remember what his name was. He just sat there watching the water; never once looked up. I don't think he even saw us. But then just before we were about to go, he gets up takes all his clothes off and jumps in. I shouted but dad just told me to shut up. He said it'd be no harm if the likes of him were to drown anyway.

He was one of those lads that I always tried to keep away from. If one of his crowd saw me they'd start calling my specky and saying I was getting shagged by the PE teacher. Sometimes at break I'd watch them all messing around in the bag room. All of them piling in there with a load of girls, all shouting and laughing and feeling each other up and that.

I suppose they did that so that no one knew whose hand was whose, who was touching who. Once they dragged one of the girls from our year in, she had no choice. I wanted to go over and rescue her, like I was some brave GI rescuing a French woman from the hands of some SS man. I could see it all unfolding in my head like the pages of a commando book flicking past. I knew I couldn't of course. I knew they'd kill me if I went anywhere near them. I felt useless and I felt sorry for her.

But after that she started hanging round with them and even started going out with one of the boys. Part of me wished I could join in with them. I thought it would be the only chance I'd ever get to actually touch a girl. But I couldn't of course. Even if they'd have let me I wouldn't have been able to do it. It wouldn't have been the honourable thing. Would have been like me turning traitor, going over to the enemy. But I did want to know what it felt like, what it would be like to save a whole village of French women from certain death at the hands of the Gestapo.

I don't know why I took the first one. I suppose it was because it was there. All white and frilly with tiny patterns across the material. It was just there on its own, so I picked it up and stuffed it into my coat pocket and left as quickly as I could. God, I remember trying to get through the next lesson, just praying that no one would find it, just wanting to get home and have a closer look. I'd never have lived that one down. Well it would be another thing that I would never have lived down. I got home though and I remember just sitting there all night turning it over and over in my hands and rubbing the material across my face.

It just sort of seemed to grow from there really. Like it happened by accident. I never intended to start collecting bras. I took the next one from a shop in town. Mum was at the counter complaining about something and demanding a discount and I just slipped it into my pocket. I know stealing is wrong. That's the first and last time that I've ever taken anything from a shop. To be honest it just didn't feel right, too stiff, too rough, just not worn I suppose.

I got the rest from the same place as the first one, the lost property bin outside the school swimming pool. I wondered how the girls could have gone home without them, how they could have forgotten to put it on. But I remember once after swimming when I forgot to put my pants on. Gerry Carr overheard me asking for them back and after that everyone got shouting at me - you going commando to day, bit cold down there is it – a load of them gathered around me trying to pull my trousers down. Them all laughing as I stood there with them round my ankles - I don't know why you bother wearing pants you've got nothing to put in them - they said - perhaps you left them in Mr Kennedy's office , you like him don't you.

Mr Kennedy was the only teacher who had anytime for me. He was always asking after me. He didn't force me into doing PE. Never got harsh with me like he did with the other lads. When I'd tell him that I'd forgotten my kit he'd just raise his eyebrows and say - forgotten again hey, ok well just go to the library and wait for your next lesson. I think he sort of knew about the gip I used to get in the changing rooms; them hiding my bag and hiding my clothes and that.

After a few weeks I'd managed to get hold of quite a few bras. I kept them stashed under my bed, hidden behind a stack of Commando comics. Day by day my collection got bigger. Different colours, sizes, materials, patterns. Each one had its own special feel to it. I'd wait until mum and dad had gone to sleep, get one out from under the bed and stuff the cups full of tissue.

Putting it on I'd lie there in the dark feeling the delicate patterns, feeling the material, feeling the lovely firm breasts of Sharon Matthews.

I worked my way through all the bras. Each one a different name, a different image. But that wasn't enough though; I wanted to know what it would be like to be that GI. One night when mum and dad had gone down to the social together I knew I had my chance, one of those rare occasions when I had the house to myself. I got all of the bras out from under my bed and set about stuffing all of the cups full of tissue.

When I'd finished doing that I started to pin up a load of string to my ceiling, moving my chair around the room, climbing up and back down again until the entire ceiling was covered. I took each bra and tied a piece of string to one of the straps.

When I'd finished it was a sight to behold. All those colours and patterns surrounding me. I turned the lights out and slowly walked around my room, letting them all bang into my face, pretending that I was there in the bag room with all the girls, with Sharon Matthews, with Chloe Dean, with Angela Jones. Pretending that I was the hero in the French village. The Gestapo man dead at my feet and all the women wanting to thank me, just me, their smiles, their kisses, hugging me and holding me to their chests. It felt so good.

And then there was the snap of the light switch, a sudden explosion ripping the images apart and then the - what the fuck is going on here! - I knew it was his voice, but I couldn't see anything through the curtain of bras until his fat arms parted them in front of me. I could see mum behind him, I'll never forget the look of horror in her eyes. She stood there shaking and shouting over and over again - the dirty little brat, the dirty little brat, the filth of it, the filth of it. Dad just flipped, started ripping down all the bras from the ceiling before he started ripping into me.

Mum wouldn't look at me after that. She'd talk to dad as if I wasn't there saying - I can't understand what's going through his head, the dirty good for nothing, I told you we should have never sent him to that school, look what's happened to him, it's disgusting, it's disgusting. They made me feel like I was the first boy to ever think about some tits before, and at the time I thought that perhaps I was.

I thought that as time went on things would get a bit better, but they didn't. Mum was still breaking into floods of tears all the time and dad was spending more and more time down at the social.

I didn't think it could get any worse and then a few weeks after the incident I came home from school and found the tank empty. The Graf Spee had one of its funnels broken off and Rhubarb and Custard were gone. I knew it was him straight away but I just didn't want to believe it. I came running out of my room and he was there at the bottom of the stairs laughing and shouting that they'd gone for a swim and that would teach me, that no son of his would ever do anything like that.

And then mum was there crying and saying what have you done to his fish and him telling her to shut the fuck up, and how after all he'd done, after acting like a real father for all those years, after all the sacrifices he'd made and her saying don't you dare, don't you dare.

I ran out of the house and left them to it. I ran straight down to the river, down to the patch of waste ground and sat there for hours just staring into the water, hoping to catch a glimpse of them. I never did. Now I just like to think that somehow they managed to survive, somehow managed to swim their way out of that stinking river, somehow found themselves a nice little pond where they lived out the rest of their lives.

I've got my own tropical fish tank now. I've got Mollies, Tetras, a Fancy Guppy and some Angel Fish. All those colours keeping guard over a sunken treasure chest that's overflowing with coins and gems, all out of reach, all safe behind the glass.

I managed to get myself a job in the pet shop in town and couldn't resist buying a small round fish bowl with two ordinary goldfish. I haven't given them names. I didn't think it would be right. I don't want to grow too attached. Every now and then I take them out for a walk.

It might sound a bit strange, but why not? People take dogs for a walk, exercise horses, so I take them out once a week for a walk in town, just showing them around, showing them how nice their little bowl really is, showing them that I keep them safe. They don't have to deal with anyone else. It's just me and them and that's the way I like it.

I even bought myself another bra. Just the one mind and I keep it well hidden in case anyone ever decides to come round and visit; you never know? I'll get it out every now and then for old time sake, squeezing hard on the tissue filled cups whilst desperately trying not to think about Rhubarb and Custard.

ADRIAN CAINES

Thank you

Thank you for the consistency of your love,
which filled me fully.
Thank you for standing beside me,
as the path turned to splinters
and crises crashed upon me.

Thank you for the sunsets and vistas
that your confidence gave me,
when my impoverished ambition
threatened to condemn me to the foothills.

Thank you for holding on to me,
when to be carried away
was the just preserve of my treachery.
Thank you for curling your arms around me,
when fevered nights stretched out like teeth.

Thank you for guiding me
past the pitfalls of opulent resentment,
for leading me from base pursuits
and inevitable scratches upon my conscience.

Thank you for the value
that I could lay claim to,
by being loved by you.
Thank you for being you,
and sharing you with me.

JONATHAN CHAMBERLAIN

The Boat

At first of course it was just a dream. The kind of dream that comes to you in the early hours of an autumnal morning after a deep and richly satisfying sleep - when the body is still supine and heavy, but replete with sleep. The mind drifts. Glorious sunny thoughts flit about. Sheer luxuriant joy.

This thought was different only in that it seemed eminently possible. All he had to do was believe in it. If he believed in it enough then he could do it. That was clear enough. Right from the beginning.

At first he smiled at the possibility. It was a joke that gently teased him. Of course it was impossible. It was much too big an idea. Too great an enterprise for such as him. What was he after all? Just a dreamer. A man who had idle dreams. But the dream somehow didn't disappear as other dreams do when the day calls and the practical business of life has to be attended to. It stayed. And the longer it stayed the more he realised that the difficulties were not insuperable. All that was required was a seemingly superhuman commitment. So the problem was not, he came to realise, the problem of doing it. The problem was in wanting enough to do it. Just having enough faith in himself. Just believing in himself. Was it possible that he could think of himself as important enough to merit the expenditure of time, energy and, yes, money? For if he did it, he would be doing it as a present to himself.

In his dream he had dreamed of building himself a boat, and taking it down to the sea and launching it and then sailing away in it. And that, ultimately, was the whole point: to sail away in it.

And one morning it came to him that he did think of himself as important enough to merit the expenditure of time energy, and, yes, even the money.

He found suddenly he had a great and pressing need for a pocket calculator so that he could while away a morning making abstruse calculations. He worked at first on the back of an envelope but then transferred these to a

32

larger piece of paper. The calculations changed depending on the assumptions he was making, so the page soon filled up with numbers and crossed out numbers and other numbers seemingly so grotesque they had been all but mutilated.

And finally, what all these numbers told him was that the plan was feasible if he really did believe in himself and he really did want this enough.

He sat still for an eternity of moments as he considered the import of what he was asking himself to do. There was still time to say no. There was still time to smile ruefully and shake his head and let the dream dribble away as other dreams had dribbled away before. He thought hard and he thought long - and wide and deep. Finally, a deep sigh escaped him. It was a sigh of reluctant acceptance. This was a day of judgement. When he was old and grey he would look back on this moment and judge himself according to the decision he now took. And it came to him he no longer had a choice. If he did nothing else in his whole life he would at least do this. He would do it just to show that he loved himself and that he was worth the effort. And because, ever since the dream had come to him, he had felt that life with the dream made sense; but that life without the dream, in the very ashes of the dream, was no longer an existence worth contemplating. It would have been filled with the failure of wanting enough to live.

And he wanted suddenly to live.

It was going to be a long project. He could see that. It was going to fill months and years of his life. "Two years," he thought optimistically. "It'll take me two years."

So he needed somewhere he could work steadily and without interruption. Somewhere he could leave his tools without any fear that they would go missing. Somewhere large. And no sooner had he started looking than he found it. A run down shed that had once housed goodness knows what. The owner agreed to let it out for a small sum.

Even then the dream might have shown itself to be unfeasible. It was possible there was a small part of his brain that secretly hoped there would be an obstacle so large that it would confront him with the majestic absurdity of his ambitions. An obstacle so bluntly immovable that he would not be able to blame himself for his failure to continue. He could retire from the fray with honour enhanced, no stain of failure needing to be hidden.

But each obstacle fell away even as he approached it. He ordered the design and it came. He was going to build a catamaran. Twenty-eight feet long. A ship that could take him across oceans. He bought the tools and found a wood supply. Then came the problem of glue. He found that the glue he needed was only available by direct order in commercial quantities from abroad. He enquired if they would agree, in his case, to consider a smaller order. A reply came back. They would. Then he had to wait. Finally it arrived. Everything was ready. He could start.

He worked slowly, with the infinite, inexorable patience of the man who has no fears of arriving but who wishes the moment of arrival to be total and complete. And it was true, now that the work had started, that he no longer had any fears. He felt rather a warm glow in his belly. At first it was barely noticeable but as the work progressed it grew more intense and spread. It manifested itself in the spring of his step and the light in his eyes. He was in command of his own fate.

There were to be no last minute worries suddenly that this section or that part had been skimped on or was wanting in any manner. He asked questions of himself and the design and made modifications as he went along. He imagined how life aboard his boat would be in the roaring, growling oceans and he added supports and rope holds and discovered ways of strengthening the frame. Of course he had to work at his full-time job to get the money to afford the wood and paint and glue and ropes and sails and all the rest of it. The project inched forward with infinite slowness.

At first friends and neighbours looked on with a nod of respect. Respect gave way to mild humour. The size of the commitment was so vast. Surely he had taken on too much. Maybe he had. Sometimes he thought that too, mocking himself. But he felt that glow in his belly. He had no fears on that score. News became folklore. That's the barn where the boat is being built. Winter became spring passed through summer and autumn and returned to winter and continued through to the soggy dampness of spring again. That's the barn where the boat is being built. Oh yes? I've heard of that. Summer became autumn and winter came again, the season of fingerless mittens. Folklore became myth. If the gods want to destroy you, they first convince you to build a boat.

But it continued to progress - as if the very future itself was hauling it forward to completion. But this was not a piece of work that could be hurried. He did not want a boat that leaked. But all boats leak his sailing friends assured him. Yes, he knew that. But he wanted a boat that didn't leak. And always there were the over-riding concerns of balance and symmetry. The two hulls needed to be laboriously caulked. It took time and patience. A lot of patience.

Brass fittings were purchased from chandler's shops in narrow alleys. These shops outfitted working boats. He felt increasingly at home here surrounded by the brass lanterns and rope and fishing tackle and bales of canvas sheeting. This was his world. Then there were the sails. They too had to be ordered from abroad. And when they came they had to be inspected inch by inch.

It all took much longer than he had expected. Jobs that he had imagined might take days took months. Two years stretched into three. Three years sweated into four. Four years groaned into five.

And then, one day, it was damn near finished.

The boat was ready to be brought out of the shed and taken down to the water and floated. He saw himself getting on, pulling up the sail and just sailing away into the deep vast solitude of the empty ocean.

Escape. This after all was the ultimate purpose. Beyond the escape there was nothing. He had no dreams of arriving in foreign ports. His dream considered only the leaving. Soon. Very soon. This was the moment to allow the first subtle tingling quivers of anticipation to flutter in his stomach.

He opened the doors of the shed and looked out. It was late afternoon and expecting to be dazzled by the rays of the setting sun, he half-closed his eyes. He wanted to bathe himself in the cleansing rays, to be purified by the light. Instead he was enveloped in dark shadow. Puzzled, he opened his eyes and looked around. He thought he knew this place. But the world had moved on. Where before there had been a grassy wasteland there was now a block of flats. It stood obstinately in his way. In his mind he had seen himself drag the boat from the shed, across the empty space and into the water of the bay. But now a building stood in his way. He would have to take it another way. He looked to the right. There was another block. Just as flat and solid and mutely obstinate. To the left there was another block. He was hemmed in by blocks. In every direction buildings had somehow risen up where before there had only been the desolate openness of space that served no use. What had been scrubland littered with old paint cans and bent rusty nails now reverberated to the deep, resonating, half-suppressed sounds of human existence.

How could he not have seen it happening? How could he not have heard it? This low yet somehow vast murmuring of people. He could feel it vibrate in the ice-cold chambers of his belly. Children shrieked. Clothing flapped from washing lines. Caged birds whistled piercing, disconnected, haunting notes.

And as he looked around in stunned, numbed, bemusement, he murmured to himself: "Well, I'll be damned."

MOSS RICH

After surgery in a Brighton hospital

After hearing a blast of hymn tunes through the ward at Sunday lunchtime, a smallish, plumpish, greyish man came into the ward pushing a trolley with a musical appliance blaring out a non-denominational hymn tune. The hymn was "The rich man in his castle / The poor man at his gate / God made them high and lowly / And ordered their estate". I knew it well from the morning assemblies of my schooldays. Whenever there was some political upheaval in the land our hymns master, who was also the organist, would choose this hymn to assure the boys that everything was under divine control and we need not worry our young heads about the political situation. Our visitor came to each bed and shook hands with each of us. He mumbled something I could not understand, to which I responded heartily 'and the same to you, Sir', which I thought was quite safe.

I finished the meal of personal choice, which had been ordered by the previous occupant of my bed, then reached to my bedside cabinet for pen and paper. I then sketched out the following.

The rich man from his castle,
The lowly at his gate –
And one might have a hernia,
The other a poor prostate.

The rich men may get richer,
The lowly higher climb,
But none will have the wit to dodge
The languid creep of Time.

Time is a wordless insult,
It spins a spidery mesh
And – snaring us poor, hapless flies –
Humiliates the flesh.

But still the final friendship,
For time is on their side
Whose groans have agonised the ward
At last, when they have died.

Daughter of Wenceslas

For R – a lady in one of our literary group who adds excellence to our discussions of English poetry. Born and brought up in the Czech Republic, she came here to study English and stayed on. Her command of our language is equal to that of the Queen's English, and is probably better than that of some of the Queen's family. 'Bring me flesh and bring me wine, bring me pine logs hither…'

Peasants are we from the frosts of the woodlands,
Foraging warmth for our souls in the good lands.
Shrouded in darkness our minds as our bodies
Groping the air to discover where God is.

Bent low in peasanthood, lost for encouragement,
Peers none from the castle, bearing us nourishment?
Ah! Lifting our eyes to the skies to assist us
Sing the Lord's praises, the angels have kissed us.

Here in the midst of us, none to escort her,
In an aura of grace, it is Wenceslas' daughter!

As fine Thought is food for the senses she hastens
To bring us the finest from Fortnum and Mason's.
Tastefully packaged in wisdom her language is
Rich with the relish of smoked salmon sandwiches
With honoured-guest dishes from our day to feudal,
Soup of red beetroot with sauerkraut and strudel.
And the fragrance! The fragrance that makes the heart quicken,
How wishful the bone, how tender the chicken.
And picked from the vineyard with fingertip care,
The sweetest of grapes from a notable year.

The food from the fridge that K. Wenceslas emptied
He shared with Joe Peasant with nothing exempted.
So too our dear mentor whose Thought-generosity
Is boundless yet never is marred by verbosity.
Unfailing she gives us the meanings of meanings
Great poets have penned where we have only gleanings.
Unfailing she sees it her God-given mission
Upholding beneficent Royal tradition.
As when King to commoner "M'sieur let me offer yer
This scrumptious peanut dreamt up by Escoffier",
And draining a glass of a vintage Chianti,
The King to our Joey, "M'sieur, votre santé "

Daughter of Wenceslas, Princess Bohemia,
Vous êtes la crème de la crème, only creamier.

ALASDAIR CRAIG

Sky's the limit

If, when I was young, I had owned a magic lamp, I would have asked my genie to grant me the gift of flight - seamless, effortless flight, like that of a bird. Of course I gave up wishing as I grew older, because like most children who make wishes on magic lamps, the genie I summoned came out swinging and laughed in my face.

Although I have come to accept that I will never fly like a bird, the wishes I made in childhood, were made before I had the knowledge that they already lay broken, and these are the most stubborn of dreams that always leave a stain. At school I was encouraged to pursue metaphorical flight, through learning. I was told that with an education "the sky would be the limit" and that "anything would be made possible" to me, with all the power it provided: a good job and money was the world's counter offer to my impossible childhood hopes. The only person I have ever talked to about my desire to fly is my best friend, James. During the wee hours of a particularly messy stag do, he had suggested that I take flying lessons. I had a good job and could afford it, but it would be an inadequate substitute. I explained to him that it was all or nothing for me and that planes where just airborne wheelchairs for creatures who had no business in the sky.

As a kid I used to want to grow up to become a milkman because it meant that I didn't have to wear a seat belt; but my job title nowadays is 'Executive Overseas Sales Co-ordinator'. As an 'Executive Overseas Sales Co-ordinator' I have toured around the world, but I have only seen the parts that aren't worth seeing and all I ever bring back is business proposals and single-use bars of soap. I sometimes wonder if I would have been better off as a milkman.

The snow was still thick on the ground and all flights had been delayed until further notice. I was smoking, out of boredom, in the airport's outside courtyard, when I saw the pigeon swoop down, but if I hadn't seen it with my own eyes then I would have found it hard to believe such a mangy creature could fly at all. It was blackened with dark slicks and fluffy as a clog in the vacuum cleaner. The planes were all tucked up in their hangers, yet this flimsy looking creature could still fly. It had found a coal-like lump that must have once been food, which it mined from time to time for some forgotten nourishment.

By now the snow had already detained me for two hours in Houston Airport, but the lady at the flight desk had said that the runways were being cleared and a few other airlines were getting flights out. Not that at this late hour there was anyone around to care. Most of the other passengers had left, choosing to wait until tomorrow when normal service should be resumed. It seemed that now the airport's employees outnumbered its passengers, late night radio favourites chimed from the speaker system. The music very apparent now due to the lack of background noise, 10 tons of unfilled space drifted in every direction.

As an 'Executive Overseas Sales Co-ordinator' I had a ticket that gave me access to the airport's Executive Lounge. My experience has shown me that executive lounges are in general characterless affairs, embellished just enough with stylish designer furniture to be comfortable, but not cared-for enough to be interesting or homely. Houston Airport's Executive Lounge was no exception. It was as if an interior designer and a low-cost construction firm had eaten some flat-pack furniture and then shat it out at random around a room. But even at this late hour they would sell you a drink and provide you with a chair.

It was pretty dead when I entered, a few suits like myself tapping at their Blackberries over suitcases and a greying forty-something in casual sports wear (as the catalogues call it), at the bar. He appeared to be trying to persuade the bar lady to have a drink with him. I approached and she broke away from the conversation to serve me. I ordered some food and beer and then retreated to a quiet corner to spend some time in a form of solitude, but it was no good. I waited there for forty minutes with no news of the flight and only the performance of the man at the bar to watch. I grew restless and wandered for awhile.

I entertained myself by going back and forth on a moving walkway, then watched from a large glass window as a few planes taxied around pointlessly, huge and ungraceful as they roared and lumbered. I thought again of the mangy pigeon and its unbelievable powers of flight. Then came an announcement over the tannoy informing me that the delayed 23.07 to Gatwick would be ready to take off in an hour.

My ticket gave me access to the first class seating on the plane. Back in the days before I was an 'Executive Overseas Sales Co-ordinator', in the days when I was a simple 'Sales Co-ordinator', I was impressed by the idea of first class travel and the executive lounge, but I know now that people who use the airlines frequently often come to hate it, just as, in my roll as 'Executive Overseas Sales Co-ordinator', I had come to hate flying. It was a chore to me, a place between two destinations where I spent hours at a time. I now see the first class seating and the executive lounge as tools to help me fend off the deep vein thrombosis my life style has been known to create.

The first class section of the delayed 23.07 to Gatwick had seats that were divided into sets of two, so that each passenger only shared a row with one other person - and I have met some bizarre travelling companions this way - sat next to the best of them: concert pianists, body guards, even a famous puppeteer. When I sit next to someone like that I am ashamed to tell them that I am an 'Executive Overseas Sales Co-ordinator', so I prefer to sit next to some boring bastard who runs out of conversation ten minutes into the journey and shuts up for the rest of the flight. But it's a lucky dip as to who you will encounter - cast your hook in to a large enough pool of human life and you are bound to pull out a weirdo from time to time. I recognised my travelling companion as soon as he approached my row, it was the man I had noticed at the bar earlier and I had a feeling that he was looking for the seat next to mine.

"Hi" he began, in a broad Texan accent. "I'm Chris".

I took his hand and introduced myself. Now that he was closer to me I had a better chance to examine him. His face was covered in patches of flaky skin and one of his ears looked as though it had been freshly pierced, with a slim rim of blood around a gold hoop earring which had all the subtlety of a wound to the face.

"You British?" he questioned enthusiastically.

"I am" I told him, against my better judgement.

"Tell me," he continued, "Can people still smoke in bars over there?"

"No. It's similar laws to most of America now." I confirmed.

He swore to himself, then announced, "That's a shame. I was in Seoul a few weeks ago and you can still smoke over there. You can even smoke in an elevator for God's sake!" He rubbed his chin, dislodging a few flaky bits of skin that floated in the air around his face. "Do you travel a lot?"

I told him of my duties as an 'Executive Overseas Sales Co-ordinator' at which he grew visibly more animated,

"Get out of town!" he roared, I'm an Executive Overseas Sales Co-ordinator too! I work for Peterson and Bower, the 9th largest distributor of industrial quality rubber in the US!" We exchanged views on the job for a while, before he leaned in close and said with meaty breath, "You know, with this job, I've gotten sick of flying."

"Yeah," I said, and somehow I felt a relief in saying "I can't stand it any more either."

"You know what", he said to me, "I hate this fucking airline food." It seemed that it was therapeutic for him also, "Don't matter how much you pay for your ticket it always gives me gas. I just take a couple of doses of Tylenol before I leave nowadays, and sleep through the journey."

By now the airport was but a light in the distance, the ground glowed with the eerie light of the snow's reflection.

"So, you're going to London on business then, I take it?" I asked Chris.

"Oh no, not this trip. I'm going to meet a lady." He produced a picture from his pocket of a beautiful dark haired girl and showed it to me. "Alyona, met her on the internet. She's Russian," he added, and raised one eyebrow boastfully.

"Oh, so she lives in London?"

"No Russia, we just decided to meet in a neutral place. It's quite a standard thing to do when you meet girls from the internet - you know, to make sure you're not a fruit cake or something."

"Of course," I said, unsurely, "So you do this a lot - meet women off the internet, I mean?"

"Oh yeah, man. I'll tell you, there's no better way to pick up chicks than the internet. There may be cheaper ways, but if you ask me it's worth every penny, man. I mean just look at this girl!" he jabbed a finger at her picture again, "You see it's always been my ambition to fuck as many beautiful women as I can."

"Is that so?" I said, a bit taken aback.

"Fuck pretty girls, you know, as many as possible. That's my dream, man! See, I only ever had three goals in my life: one is to make money - got that; two is to own a Ferrari - got that; and the third is to fuck beautiful girls - and now I got that!" He leaned in close again and said in a quieter voice, "About ten months ago I had a heart attack on this dude's ranch in Kansas, but since then I learned something: Life's short, man - you got to chase your dreams or die with regrets."

Chris went on in this manner for about ten more minutes before the Tylenol began to kick in and he eventually drifted off to sleep. I entertained myself by watching the film *Wild Hogs*, a film so bad it made me angry so I had to stop watching. About two hours into the flight Chris started snoring. After about four hours he started farting, making smells that no healthy man should make, so I looked out the window for a bit in a attempt to keep my face away from these detonations. It was still dark outside but a slice of sun had just started to appear, dusting the tops of the ice cream scoop clouds with a yellow tint on one side, and for a while I was lost in its beauty.

I'm glad that my dream is unachievable, because if Chris had achieved his dream, then I wanted none of it. A man not so dissimilar to me, whose near-death experience on a dude's ranch in Kansas had awoken his dying rock and roll dreams, who may well have thought that everyone loves a Ferrari, but who had forgotten that everyone hates Ferrari drivers. I felt glad that although I was flying, my childhood wish was to fly like a bird, not just to look out the window of a plane next to a farting sex tourist, and not even a heart attack at a dude's ranch could change that for me. I am proud to have an impossible dream. People might think is silly to wish for things that won't come true, but if a dream is achievable then you're not dreaming hard enough, and in a world where every fool wishes for wisdom, the wise give up their wishes.

SIAN EVANS

Brighton, a love story

In love like Parnel and Kitty O'Shea
Young men now hold hands and gaze at the sea
Where the pier, like Miss Havisham's wedding cake
Still on its legs in that urgid lake,
Is mouldering quietly with the same discretion
That we commit our weekly transgression.
O my love, tall and proud, and from Worthing-on-Sea
It's a wife that you leave when you come visit me.
Safe bungalow-land where the net curtains twitch
That you flee from to soothe your primordial itch.
In Norfolk Square one wino sips
Some strange sad song is on another's lips
I hurry past towards that sweet sharp shock
When I shall greet you by the floral clock
And then I'll kiss your rain washed face
In your warm dark car and in disgrace
well go to the hotel near the Royal Pavillion
Now restored at the cost of several million,
And after that last cigarrette
I see, like Mr Wilde, that your lashes are wet.

I wouldn't trade Brighton with all its piers
and all its queers and its racketeers
And its Proustian ladies whose canine friends
On Hove seafront walks make daily amends
For Loves they had when they were young and free
Loves who came from Worthing-On-Sea.

Beautiful Baby

Beautiful baby, living on looks
If you say maybe, I'll buy you some books
Don't want you to read them, Please don't get wise
Or that innocent look will be gone from your eyes...
I've seen some lookers, they come and go
But never a vision that haunted me so
So much to tell you but nothing to say,
Don't wanna spoil you lookin that way
Watchin your lashes when your asleep
I'm just in heaven, heart skips a beat
And just to see you at break of day
You fill my vision,what can I say
You've no social skills, ain't got no heart
You're just a fabulous work of art
I know beauty's costly and I'll pay the bill
But not just yet cos you're with me still,
There'll be another, richer than me
Babe I'm not stupid and I'll set you free
Dont want to lose, but I ain't no fool
There'll be no crying, that wouldn't be cool

    But don't ever change
    Please don't you change.

An Italian love affair

The mountains rose before us
Then, as we crested the Corniche
The sea, pale marbled milk, trailed behind
As we drove on.
Upwards into dusk, a faery sky whose tresses were veiled
Lost in another language.
And then later
A white mosquito net flowed down on to a blood red bed
Your dark face above me, tender as the night...
afterwards, you turned a different face towards me
"Solo amiccis", you told me
"Io sono libre. Sempre."
and I replied "always". More coming-light going.

The merman

I swam in the sea, all wreathed in mist
The water silken as a milk lagoon
The beach as empty as the day wed kissed
another summer. now returned too soon.
Ah, to sink beneath the dreamless waves
where ancient sailors bones are found
And wait amidst their watery graves
and meet a merman in the fronded gloom
Whose skin is of silvery fishes scales
And whose eyes are cobalt blue
Who tells one charming ocean tales
None of which are true.

The death of Stuart Slade

We were lost and committed
Nothing we could not do
So the pea green boat we kitted
With plenty of things to do
A guitar, honey and a little weed,
Some oars and some beautiful snow white sails
So the craft would respond when the wind breathed speed
We'd choose a soft night with a ribbon of moon
Towards the horizon wed sail
Crack open champagne, I'd play you a song
Watching sea horses silvery pale.
We'd laugh at the world as we'd be long gone
We'd never look back at that dismal charade
Kiss as we pulled the pin of the hand greanade
And stand in the boat, Phoenicians at last
As the craft, you and I flashed red from the blast
I wish, how I wish that we'd done that one night
How superbly our destiny would have been designed.

But, alas, that fate was not to be
You were stabbed in the street, coming to me
Because you were tall he came from behind
Never you saw for your tears made you blind.
You fell. Black blood in the street
Your sweet throat pale. my heart in bed beat
To miss you forever, Why couldn't it be
That we'd died together in the moonlit sea.

ROB PARAMAN

From Having the Glide

Franger was obviously winning in the fight for Kayleigh. I pondered over how I was going to claw my way back. Homework was against my religion and so was Christianity but I figured that if Franger could outsmart me on the homework front then I could out Christianise him on the spiritual front.

I went to the Billebellary Op Shop and bought a silver cross on a chain for twenty-five cents. The cross was about two inches long - a good quarter inch bigger than Franger's. I found my old black shoes at the back of my wardrobe. They were tight on me now but I only had to wear them for a few hours. I gave them a polish then I ironed my dacks. I even neatly combed my hair. I fastened the silver chain around my neck and positioned the cross outside of my tucked in and ironed shirt.

I felt like shit.

I went to the bathroom and grinned at the born again dag in the mirror. I looked like shit. I said cheesily, "Now go forth and multiply – Chapter ten – verse eight – Corinthians."

At twenty past ten a.m. the church car park was full. I spotted the Skerrett's Valiant in the corner.

As I squeaked into the chapel I saw the Skerretts on the front pew. But there was no sign of Kayleigh.

'Maybe her family trusts Franger so much he's allowed to sit with Kayleigh somewhere alone, away from the family?'

Out of the the corners of my eyes I scanned the congregation but neither Kayleigh nor Lover Boy were anywhere to be seen. Reverend O'Leary, at the front asked us to turn to Hymn number something or rather. I opened my hymnbook anywhere. Everyone started singing away and I mimed along. Then it dawned on me, 'Kayleigh and Franger must be going to the fucking evening service! But I can't just leave now, the Skerretts and the Billebellary gossips will put two and two together. The only thing to do now is think and wait and fast through this whole nightmare and earn some brownie points in the process.'

Next thing an old man's wrinkly hand appeared and took my hymnbook away from me and handed me another hymnbook that was opened at the correct page. The old do-gooder smiled condescendingly at me and I smiled and nodded a silent, 'thank you' as if I was a thicko.

After a few hymns with my next-door neighbour checking over my shoulder each time to see that I had found the right page Reverend O'Leary said, "Now, let us pray!"

As he babbled away I was feeling more and more restless. 'While I'm stuck in here getting lip service from Reverend O'Leary, Franger is out there getting tongue service from Kayleigh Skerrett. Where's the fairness in that? – God? Please, God, if you really do exist – prove it by moving Franger down to D grade and bringing Bluey back up to C grade. As you saw yourself, God, Franger stole two bucks fifty from the Children's Hospital collection box and he never ever got punished for it. Amen.'

Reverend O'Leary began his sermon on The Power Of Belief. After a while I began to appreciate Einstein's theory of relativity. For every ten minutes spent in church only one minute would pass on my watch face. I then noticed a fly buzzing overhead. It landed on the ear of one of the Johnson twins. He waved it away and it flew over and landed on Mrs. Cruikshank's hat and then over to the vase of flowers at the front.

Auntie Marg once told me an old Buddhist proverb –

'An order of Buddhist monks had all gathered in their temple for a lecture from their Master. A bird appeared on the windowsill and the master sat there for a while watching the bird. All the monks began watching the bird, too. The bird flew away and the Master pressed his palms together and said, "That is the end of today's lesson." He then got up and left.'

I couldn't see that happening in 1977 in an Australian Church with a fly and a Reverend. Only a plague of locusts could get us out of this one. Above Reverend O'Leary, at the front wall, up near the ceiling, was a little arched stained glass window of Jesus with his delicate hands outstretched. There were other stained glass windows along the sides of the chapel but they were of deep blues and reds. The Jesus window was of bright gold and orange with sections that were of clear glass. The fly flew across to him and bumped head on into the windowpane. I was the only one who heard the sound. It flew off again, back around the church, surveying the area for an escape. Then he flew up straight back into it again. Unable to get through - off he went for yet another lap around the chapel. This became a continuous cycle but each journey of exploration got shorter and shorter and he always flew back to

Jesus' open arms - smack bang into the glass again. Eventually he remained at the window for good and went into a buzzing frenzy all around the periphery of the window.

Reverend O'Leary said, "Now, let us open our Hymn books to number seventy one – Open the Windows Of Heaven."

I knew the do-gooder standing next to me was looking over my shoulder so I flicked through the pages to Hymn number seventy-one. Pointing to the correct number I turned to him with a saccharine sweet smile.

As I sang along I saw the fly pace straight across Jesus' face. Jesus didn't flinch or give it the Aussie salute. He just kept on gazing straight ahead over his flock. There was more life in that little fly than in all those stained windows and the Sistine Chapel and the Taj Mahal put together. The fly started dancing angrily around the windowsill again.

'It's a shame,' I thought, 'Why don't they leave that little window open an inch or two during the service?' But then I noticed that the window had no latch or hinges. That window would always be closed. Devadatta would never allow this sort of thing to happen at the temple.

When we finished singing we all sat down and Mr. Skerrett went and opened the big arched doors. He was instantly silhouetted by pure white sunlight. A cool breeze swept through the chapel. I breathed a sigh of relief knowing that the service would soon be over. But we had one more song to sing to earn our freedom. It was Hymn number one three eight, called, 'Jesus Is The Only Way.' To please the old codger next to me I turned to the correct page and showed it proudly to him with my born again Christian sunbeam smile. To wind him up I then turned my Hymnbook upside down. He looked at me as if to say, 'Smart arse.'

We sang, "No other way! No other way!
No other way to get to heaven!
Jesus is the only way!"

I looked up to the fly at the window. Telepathically, I beckoned, 'Come this way now! There is another way out of here!'

He was still intermittently buzzing around the window frame then pacing across the glass, expecting to find an opening at any moment.

'We'll both probably die virgins.'

"No other way!
No other way!
No other way to get to heaven!
Jesus is the only way!"

'Fly, look behind you! There's even a big exit sign above the doorway! Look! That exit is a thousand times bigger than that little window and for as long as this Chapel stands that window will never ever ever open!"

He wasn't listening. He could see the light with his own thousand eyes. Not a single doubt crossed his mind as to where his salvation lay.

"No other way!

No other way!
No other way to get to heaven!
Jesus is the only way!"
I was singing along but I swapped the words around on the last line. Instead of singing, "Jesus is the only way," I sang,
"Jesus is only in the way."
People were shuffling past me to the doorway. But I couldn't take my eyes off the fly.

I could have knocked down the other three walls of the chapel with a fucking sledgehammer and that little fly's faith would still be unshaken. He was sticking to what he believed in. I was tempted to ask Reverend O'Leary for a ladder so that I could climb up and guide him through the open doors. But Reverend O'Leary would no doubt think I was mad and Mr. Cruikshank would probably see me.

"Are you saying a prayer?"
I turned from Jesus to Reverend O'Leary.
"Um, yeah."
I looked around us. The Reverend and I were the only ones left – apart from the fly.

"I didn't want to disturb your prayer, young man, but we need to lock up the chapel now."

As we walked through the big wooden doors he closed and locked them with an enormous key. He said, "Just now with your eyes raised up to Jesus, you looked to be having a revelation!"
"I think I did have one of those, Reverend!"
He smiled, "Good to hear it. There's a lot of power in belief, you know."
"Too right!"
When he was out of sight I called back through the big keyhole, "Fly! You can crawl out through here during the night!"
As I walked around to the front of the Chapel I looked up and saw my little mate still buzzing his life away against the glass.
'I'm going to get you out of there!'
I found a sizable yonnie in the church garden. 'Stand back from the window!'
I was about to piff it at the window.
"Oi! What the hell dya think ya doin?"
It was Mister Cruickshank running from his car.

•   •   •

There was another mishap at the temple. As a part repayment for my former sins I agreed to do some chores for Devadatta while he was away for the day. He took me upstairs to his small flat.

I sat on the couch. On the coffee table in front of me was a list of the things he wanted doing. He then went into his kitchen to prepare some green tea.

I read the list. It had been written with a calligraphy pen.

'Wash dishes (properly).

Vacuum lounge and bedroom (close kitchen door, vacuum vibrations distress Gregor).

Wash prayer flags (ON GENTLE CYCLE ONLY!)

Attend to Gregor every fifteen minutes.'

I could hear Devadatta's soothng voice in the kitchen talking to someone or something.

"Daryl will be taking good care of you while Daddy is away! Oh, don't be upset Daddy will be back in a few short hours with a special treat from the park."

Devaddata returned to the lounge with a tray with a small teapot on it and two tiny cups without handles. He placed the tray on the coffee table.

"Are you good with pets Daryl?"

"Yeah, I love animals! I've got a greyhound called Govinda!"

"Come into the kitchen while the tea brews. But don't make any sudden movements, Gregor is very wary of strangers!"

My eyes wandered around the kitchen floor looking for a cat or a dog or a mouse or a rat or a guinea pig or a rabbit or a snake or a lizard but there was nothing there.

Devadatta looked into space and announced cordially, "Daryl this is Gregor – Gregor this is Daryl."

I looked a bit higher for a budgie or a cockatoo or a gold fish but there was no sign of any pets - not even a sea monkey.

"Is Gregor – is he invisible?"

Devadatta looked furious. He pointed to a piece of paper on the kitchen table.

I went, "What?"

"There look!"

There was a fly standing in the middle of a piece of paper.

"What?"

Devadatta exhaled through his nostrils.

"What - the fly?" I asked.

Devadatta seethed, "Yes! The fly is Gregor - Gregor - the human is Daryl!"

"Why don't you just get an Ant Farm?"

I took a closer look. The fly started buzzing angrily with all its might but strangely it didn't take off.

"Is he stuck there?"

"Yes, it's fly paper – it's very sticky – so don't touch it will you?"

"Fly paper? Why didn't you just swat it?"

Devadatta covered his mouth with both hands, "Daryl, when I was ordained in Nepal I made a vow not to ever purposefully kill another living thing."

"Then why have fly paper here then?"

"I can't have Gregor buzzing all around my flat spreading germs everywhere! I made a vow to maintain the highest standards of cleanliness."

"But that fly will die a horrible death stuck there on that horrible paper!"

"He will not! I take very good care of him! Don't I Gregor? He get's three square meals a day! He gets a balanced diet."

"What does he eat?"

"Don't ask! - Let's just say Gregor and I are big on recycling…"

"Eeeaw!"

"While I'm away Daryl, in fifteen minutes from now, I want you to turn Gregor's paper around ninety degrees in a clockwise direction so that he is facing the east."

"Why? Is does he pray to Allah?"

"No! He gets bored looking out that same old window all of the time. Every fifteen minutes he must be turned ninety degrees. He likes a change of scenery. Just think of yourself in his position."

"If I was in his position I'd want to be swatted with my Uncle Ted's scuff to put me out of my misery!"

"I'll be back in an hour or two."

I loaded the prayer flags into the washing machine, making triple sure I had it on the fucking gentle cycle. The prayer flags consisted of long white strings with colourful triangular flags sewn all along them. Each flag had prayers in Sanskrit hand written on them with a special calligraphy brush. I added a bit of detergent and a dash of bleach and switched it on. I went to the kitchen and washed his dishes PROPERLY.

I looked at the clock above the oven but all of the hands had been removed. I checked my watch. "Gregor, it's time for a bit of excitement!"

I turned him ninety degrees and he gave out a buzz of appreciation. I took a very close look at him. "I know just how you feel, Gregor. All revved up with no place to go! Stuck in this material world. Mind you! You must have done some very bad shit in your previous life to deserve this! You were probably a hit man in the mafia who poured the cement shoes for your enemies."

I went and opened the window. "With a bit of luck, Gregor, a female fly will fly in here and land right in front of you – facing east! No-o-o!"

I corrected myself, "That would make things even worse for you!"

I slammed the window shut. "I could tell you my life story, Gregor! - But that wouldn't be fair on you either - having no escape - and not being able to block your ears. Anyway, you're probably busy right now contemplating your own life in this cruel transient world. Just think and wait and hold fast! I'm sure tomorrow will be a better day!"

Gregor let out two positive sounding buzzes but deep down I couldn't see it happening.

The washing machine rumbled to a halt. As I unravelled the prayer flags from the machine I noticed that they were now all of a similar greyish hue. I looked in the empty machine but the prayers were nowhere to be seen.

Devadatta entered his flat and lifted a portion of the flag for inspection. His face went deep red and he looked exactly how he always looked when he chanted the word 'om' in the temple - only on this occasion he sounded the word, "Fu-u-u-u-uk!"

I went, "The Sanskrit prayers have all journeyed down the drain to join with the sea to spread throughout the world!"

"I spent months painting those prayers on!"

He lifted the bottle of bleach.

"That's why it's all ruined! Can't you read?"

He pointed to a notice written in a strange and mysterious foreign language taped above the washing machine.

I asked, "How is anyone meant to understand that?"

"Sanskrit is the most ancient and perfect language in the world."

"Well, it's perfectly useless here in Melbourne in 1977!"

He started hyperventilating. He stabbed his finger at each Sanskrit word as he read out loud, "WARNING! DO NOT USE FUCKING BLEACH WHILST WASHING PRAYER FLAGS!"

"Does it really say 'fucking?"

"No! There is no Sanskrit word for 'fucking.' I just added that in now because I am fucking angry right now!"

He slapped his forehead really hard with those last four words. He flashed a scarey grin, went to his drawer and took out his little dropper bottle of Rescue Remedy. He unscrewed the top, threw it to the floor and started dousing his naked tongue with the neat solution. He grimaced manickly as if he'd just downed a triple shot of whisky then he sputtered, "All that work I put into painting those prayers – all just vanished!"

"Nothing leaves this world, Devadatta, and nothing is ever added to the world! You told me that. All those coloured inks and all that Sanskrit wording has all just been rearranged!"

"How would you like me to rearrange your fucking face?!"

Devadatta gripped his own mouth with both hands as if something evil had just escaped from it. He sucked air in through his nostrils for two minutes til he regained his composure.

"Look at Gregor! I've never seen him so depressed! And he should be looking out the west window by now!"

Gregor let out a suicidal buzz.

Devadatta quickly turned his paper ninety degrees.

I pointed over to the sink, "Look at all your dishes! They're sparkling!"

Devadatta went over and sniffed at them, "You didn't bleach them too did you?"

In an eerie calmness Devadatta said, "Daryl, listen to me! It's been a great priveledge for me to watch your wisdom grow so deeply in this temple over the last two years one month and seventeen days! But there comes a time in every yogi's life when he must ask himself, 'Am I not now ready to find my own path out there in the world!'"

"I don't understand, Devadatta?"

He pointed to a bonsai tree on his windowsill. "If that orange tree's roots were not bound that tree would fill this entire room. It can be just the same with Yogis who have immense potentials but are constricted in small temples! Small temples like this one!"

"But I'm happy here."

He cleared the prayer flags that were covering his desk and took up a white pebble. He held it out before me in his open palm. "If you can snatch this pebble from my palm, Daryl, it will mean that you are spiritually superior to me and that you are ready now to find your own path in the world. Do you think you can do it?"

"I'll do my best, Davadatta."

I took some deep breaths and placed both palms at my hips like a gunslinger ready to draw. I looked deeply into Devadatta's eyes. My right hand flew up but I knocked the underside of his hand catapaulting the pebble across the room. I went,"Oh, damn! It looks like I'm going to be lifer here at your temple!"

Devadatta frantically searched the floor for his pebble. "Let's make it two out of three!"

•   •   •

On Monday our class went for an excursion to the Museum. Sitting on the train beside Bluey I was feeling shit.

An old posh bloke in a black suit was showing us around the Museum.

A whole corner of the museum was dedicated to aborigines. There was a life-size family of cement aborigines standing in the middle of a room-sized desert. The whole family was smiling. The father had two dead goannas hanging from his string belt. The curator drew our attention to the little bag that the mother was carrying.

"She would use that bag to gather plants and seeds," he said, "It's called a dilly bag."

He went on to explain how different tribes had different 'skin groups' that had their own totems. "For example, a man from the Yakimarr skin group may the totems of the seagull, the barramundi or the grey shark and can only marry a woman from the Bangariny skin group. The system is invaluable, especially

during drought where the different interrelated clans are obliged to help one another."
Around the outskirts of the display there were what appeared to be real gum trees.
I asked, "Are those gum trees real?"
"We have the gum tree branches replaced every two months to keep them looking fresh." The most impressive thing though was the sand that the family was standing on. It was a deep and rich orange. "Johnno asked, "Is that real sand or what?"
The curator rocked back and forward on his heels. "We had that sand carted all the way from the Nallabor Plains!"
When no one was looking I leant over the rail and nicked a hand full and stuck it in my pocket.
When Franger wasn't looking I tugged Bluey outside for a smoke. We hid behind a massive statue of a bloke on a horse spearing a dragon through the head. Right around the back of the cement plinth we met a real aboriginal couple. The bloke was wearing a battered bushies hat and a grubby Abba t-shirt and looked pissed. The woman was fast asleep in a sleeping bag on the cement. Bluey offered him a smoke and the three of us lit up.
Bluey, trying to make conversation asked, "Do you um, have one of them dilly bags?"
The aborigine laughed, "Nod ere, fella!" And pointed to a Supermarket plastic bag full of tins on the ground beside the sleeping woman.
"Is she alright?" I asked.
"Yeah, she's tired - we bin on the overnight bus from up north. Ya got two bob for flagon?"
Bluey went, "What?"
He repeated, "Ya got two bob for flagon?"
I went, "I think he wants two bob for a flagon of wine don't you?"
"Yeah, two bob for flagon."
I said to him, "But you're supposed to ask for two bob for a cup of tea!"
"I don't wanna cup o tea, brudda, I wanna flagon!"
Looking into his big brown eyes was like looking into a strange and vaste landscape. I half expected to see kangaroos and ghost gums in thier reflections.
"Yeah, but you'd have more success if you asked for 'two bob for a cup of tea.'"
"I don't wanna cup o tea. I wanna flagon!"
"My name's Daryl and this is Bluey."
We both shook his hand.
"I'm Falcon."
"See, Bluey, he's lost his land but no-one can take his totem name away from him!"

Falcon went, "Nah, Falcon's me nick name. I woz a bush mechanic up in Hermansburgh for years - had so many Ford Falcons parked round me ouse evryone started callin me Falcon!"

'Shit!' I thought, 'An aboriginal named after a bloody car! I wonder what his wife is called? – Woolworth's?'

Bluey went, "Daryl and me are both Eagle Owls!"

Falcon looked at him blankly.

I said, "They're the biggest owls in the world but we don't have them in Australia. So what are you doing down here in Melbourne?"

"We're lookin for our dorda. Guv-ment took er away from us n won't tell us where she is."

"What's her name?"

"Her name's Yani but the church named er Maria."

'Shit!' I thought, 'Maria - for an aborigine is almost as bad as Woolworth's!'

"Yani is a nice name," I said.

"Yeah, black fella word means peace."

"How old is she?"

"She'd be fifteen now. We're headin across Perth soon – lookin for me mudda too."

"You're looking for your mother, too?"

"Yeah, I last saw er when I was five."

Falcon suddenly looked as sad as fuck so I changed the subject, "You're from up north? Do you know my Auntie Marg? She's always going up there."

"To Hermansburgh?"

"No, to a place called, Laura. Is that far from Hermansburgh?"

"Not far."

"She used to show me your tribal dances and stuff but she's got a bung leg, now. Do you know her? Her name's Marg McCreedy."

"Marg? Yeah, yeah, I know Marg. She yor arnnee?"

"Yeah!"

"She owes me two bob."

"Ay?"

"Yeah, I loaned her two bob for flagon - longa time ago n she went walkabout."

"She wouldn't have been trying to diddle you, Falcon! She must have just forgotten about it! She's a bit skatty sometimes!"

Bluey added, "Sometimes?!"

I took twenty cents out of my pocket.

"Here, Falcon, let me cough up on her behalf!"

"Nah, I cooden take et!"

"No, I insist! She gets around so bloody much you might not see her again til the year two thousand and by then two bob'll be worth five cents!"

I handed him the coin and he reluctantly put it in his pocket. He took a puff on his cigarrette. "She owes me two packod o smokes, too, brudda."

We went back inside the museum. On the second floor there was hundreds of stuffed birds, the most impressive being the eagle owl. It was hanging from the ceiling on some fine fishing line. Its wings were spread to their full width of about six feet. It had massive yellow eyes. Gazing up at it together, Bluey went, "I might not be an Eagle Owl in table tennis no more but I'm still an Eagle Owl skateboarder! Nobody can take that away from me!"

The Eagle Owl's cruel tallons were out stretched, ready to snatch Bluey and I up and carry us away.

I said, "Can you imagine that, Bluey? Getting snatched away from your parents when you're just a little kid?"

The big stuffed owl had Bluey entranced, "Ha! I wonder, Daryl, did an eagle fuck an owl or did an owl fuck an eagle to produce that monster? Ha! Ha!"

"And then when you grow up you have your own kid snatched away from you as well!"

Still gawping up at the owl he said, "Ha! Ha! Did a tiger fuck a shark or did a shark fuck a tiger to produce the tiger shark?! Ha! Ha!"

"You can't hear a word I'm saying can you?"

"Ha! Ha! A shark wouldn't last long enough in a jungle to fuck a tiger! Ha! Ha!"

Bluey's laugh was starting to piss me off like never before. I asked, "How can we be doing this to all the aborigines and keep it all a big secret?"

"Ha! Ha! N a tiger'd fuckin drown tryin to fuck a shark in the ocean! Ha! Ha! Ha!"

That night I lay in bed feeling lonelier than I'd ever felt before - but not as lonely as Falcon. There was a storm outside and I started thinking about the cement aborigines in amongst the gum trees in the museum, smiling into empty space, standing on the Nallabor sand. Then my mind drifted through the museum walls, outside, to where the real aborigines were sleeping on the cement steps behind the big cement plynth.

•   •   •

Narrelle, Bluey and I sat on someone's front wall at the top of the hill.

I went, "Do you want to see me do the Dogtown Acid Drop, Narrelle?"

"What's a Dogtown Acid Drop?"

"It's when you drop from a high wall on your skateboard. Like what franger just did only I like to go a bit higher."

I stood on a section of the wall that was about four feet above the footpath. Narrelle looked well impressed. "Are you really going to drop from up there?"

I dropped to the path and polished it off with a one eighty turn. Narrelle clapped her hands and squealed, "Do it again, Daryl!"

This time I moved up to a higher section of the wall. Narrelle looked concerned but impressed, "Daryl, Ya could break ya ankles droppin from up there!"

"Life isn't worth living unless you push the boundaries!"

"Wow! You're so brave! Can you do dangerous stuff like that, Bluey?"

Bluey was lighting a cigarrette. Silently he held up his trump card - the cigarrette packet. He grinned as he tapped the bottom of the packet. In big bold letters were the words – 'SMOKING KILLS.'

How could I measure up to that?

Unfortunately the Australian Government didn't print 'SKATE-BOARDING KILLS' onto skateboards.

"Watch this, Narrelle! I called, "I'm going to try a five foot acid drop! When I land - the board could easily slip out from under me and I could easily crack my head open on the cement and die right here before your eyes!"

But Narrelle had lost interest. She was too busy watching Bluey perform a different kind of dangerous trick. He was slowly exhaling smoke out through his mouth and inhaling it back up through his nostrils. "That's amazin!" gasped Narrelle.

"It's called the Mexican Drawback," exhaled Bluey, "I get double the nicotine and if it goes around a third time I get triple!"

Narrelle put her hands to her face, "That is suicide!"

"Here I go!" I yelled, "Five feet striaght down!"

But no-one was watching. I could have Acid Dropped from a hundred feet with no parachute and no-one would have given a shit. Narrelle said to Bluey, "How long do ya think you're gunna live doin Mexican Drawbacks like that?"

Bluey shrugged casually, exhaled and spoke all at the same time, "Not long…"

She sat down on his knee and went, "Blow some smoke in me mouth n see if I can blow it out again."

"Narrelle!" I called, "I don't ever wear elbow pads or knee pads!"

Narrelle was too busy blowing the second hand smoke back into Bluey's cancerous gob.

"And only pansies wear helmets!" I called, "Watch me play chicken with the oncoming traffic!"

But it was too late. She was already pashing the guy from her own 'D' Grade caste. The Mexican Draw Backing Bluey had blown me out of town without even shifting his fat arse off the wall.

ENZO MARRA

Lifeline

Corrupt vantage,
Cruelly jests
With working pupils,
Seeing each day
Ever greyer,
Until dawn opens
Night black.

Unoriginal

You copied me,
Word for word,
Every nuance
Exactly the same,
Subtle right tilt
And no paragraph,
You even used
A red biro,
Just as
I had,
The tear at
The left corner,
Same length
And gradient,
Even though it
Ripped by chance.

Slightly Lear

Amazing tales,
Of bread and
Jam and soup,
Emerged from
Foreign lands,
All beautiful
Ad fatly proud,
They filled
Vapid lives,
With something
That resembled,
Yet didn't taste
Of hope.

Yet More Tourists

A swarm of them,
Well sunned
Dowsing themselves with beer,
With house wine
Downed delicately on streets,
White to pink
Via fleeting weekend,
Lobster bright
Like camp beacon,
A neat trick,
Until they peel
Themselves bleached.

Skinny fit

Second skin
Slid dark up,
From ankles
Bluely waist buttoned,
Rear clung,
Refused naturist
Taut seam voiced,
Street nude.

Pondering

The clouds are
Moving too slowly,
Maybe they're tired,
Taking a day off
For once,
Having a think,
A good argument
With their neighbour,
A quick wank
To relieve tension.
 Maybe their joints are
A bit creaky,
Arthritis setting in,
Their sight blurring
Out of kilter.
 Our activities below them
Growing tedious,
Small flesh bags
Scampering around,
Like freshly beheaded fowl,
Ants straining
Under Atlas predicaments,
Considering when their rain
Would most annoy.
 Resplendent in pastel serenity
Over spring sky,
They can't just
Be hanging there,
All mute
And direly numb,
That would be
Much too obvious.

Little prick

Personal burgundy vintage,
Siphoned away
As doctor ordained,
Enough for head
To swim lighten,
Cautious slow
Walk well away.

Without wave or goodbye

Five sheep
From dental flock,
Wolf stolen,
Slumbered shepherd
Dream lost useless,
Crook floor lain
In lax grip.

Mourning

Akin to funeral,
When awoken I
Will be less,
Afriad to crunch
Chew graft,
Cautious supping.

LIZ JALLA

The Blind Date

Another car-less date I muttered to myself as we walked to the restaurant, Adrian had chosen, I was cursed with them. Everyone I'd ever dated didn't drive, happened to be between cars, or, decided not to drive whenever they took me out. The last and only time I'd been driven anywhere was just after my 16th birthday, by a carrot-haired, spotty youth who I'd only agreed to go out with because of his scooter.

You'd think I'd have known by now and worn a pair of sensible shoes instead of the four inch high heels that my mother had persuaded me to buy, saying when I'd tried them on for fun, "Finally you look like a real woman."

"Lovely evening," said Adrian

It was pleasantly warm for May, with the promise of a glorious sunset when the sun sank slowly behind the trees of Greenwich Park.

"Mm," I mumbled, as I found talking distracted me from keeping my eyes peeled for anything that might trip me up. The pavements around here were known to be treacherous and I was terrified of falling over and making a fool of myself.

"I don't usually come on blind dates." Adrian tried again easily side-stepping a bin bag that having been ripped open was leaking rubbish. "But Sue kept on at my sister and she can be very persuasive, as I'm sure you know."

I was too busy avoiding the mess to answer and by the time we'd reached the downward slope Adrian had got the message and given up. It wasn't a very steep dip but in my heels it might as well have been the downward track of the big dipper.

"I'm not going down there!" I exclaimed.

"But that's the way to the restaurant," Adrian replied looking confused

"To tell the truth," I lied, "I'm not that bothered about Chinese food."

I love Chinese food but I wasn't going to admit, especially on my first date, that I hadn't mastered the art of high heels. In desperation I pointed to the Pizza parlour just across the way, full of bright lights and families with small children.

"That looks nice, why don't we go there?"

"Well I suppose.."

Without waiting for him to finish the sentence I click clacked over. The waitress showed us over to this tiny table for two squeezed in between a wall and a table occupied by a family of four. Mother, father and two children one of whom must have been deaf. For she lay sleeping across two chairs undisturbed by her sister unremitting ear-splitting scream. Slipping my feet out from their shoes I buried my face in the menu until I felt my hand being patted.

"What tits do you want?" Adrian shouted at me.

Somewhat taken aback, I looked down at my own, lying well upholstered in my new sexy super-bra. Was it so obvious that the war with gravity was all but lost? "That's personal," I shouted back, more than a bit affronted and disappointed by his remark, even if that was the sort of small talk you might expect when dating a doctor.

Looking even more confused Adrian went back to the menu. When I did the same I noticed a section under the heading Bits. Shit.

Two glasses, of what I thought was perfectly passable red wine later, I was feeling much better. My feet were no longer being tortured and after a while I sort of got used to the screams still coming from the child at the next table. Sitting back as we waited for our pizzas and garlic bread I gave Adrian my sweetest smile.

Denise had told the truth, he was good looking. Thick, brownish, grey hair that showed no signs of balding, a strong shaped jaw, I can't abide a weak chin, and blue eyes that gave me the feeling they didn't miss much. The eyes they say are the windows of the soul but I've always thought not enough value has been given to the mouth, which in my opinion can be just, and in some cases even more, revealing. I, for instance, have rather generous lips that curve upwards, which of course express my sweet, giving nature!

Having taken a swig of wine, Adrian's mouth was at the moment all puckered up as if he'd bitten into a lemon, however I'd had a chance to study it earlier and found that if I separated it from the rest of his face with the menu, and sort of screwed up my eyes till they went out of focus, his mouth looked just like Brad Pitt's, full lipped and a wee bit sulky, from which I deduced Adrian to be generous and easily hurt..

Sue had said he was in his late forties ,and though it wasn't easy to tell, under the linen shirt of a colour that perfectly matched his eyes, his body seemed in pretty good shape for his age. His arms were muscular, there was no sign of a beer-belly and his long legs didn't look bad in black jeans either. I thought, after snubbing him on our way here, that I'd better try and start up a conversation but it was impossible to get myself heard.

Fortunately we didn't have to wait long for our meal, I'd decided on the spicy chicken, Adrian went for the seafood special, you'd think being a doctor he'd have known better. Half way through our food, the family at the table opposite left, the cessation of noise made my ears pop. Eating in the sudden silence felt a bit strange like the end of *2001 Space Odyssey* when all you can hear is the main character's knife and fork scraping on the plate. Adrian didn't seem bothered, obviously too engross in his pizza to notice, so I waited till we'd finished before asking him the only lame question that came to mind.

"What made you want to be a doctor?"

A shadow passed over his face. Thinking for a moment the tee-Light in the hollowed out red plastic tomato had gone out, I checked but it was still burning.

"It's complicated," he said and refilling our glasses took a sip without hardly a pucker added "The wine's not so bad after a first glass."

Soon as we'd finished the waitress came to take our plates and sweet order. No chance of lingering between dishes here, this was a sit them down, feed them quick, then get them out, sort of place.

Still we had fun choosing, pretending to fight over the menu and changing our minds all the time, while the waitress stood there picking her spots and looking pissed off. The fluorescent lights didn't do her any favours. I was lucky Sue had come round before the date and plastered my face with enough make up to make me look radiant in a plane crash. In the end we both decided on Knickerbocker Glories and off she went.

The piped music that had been drowned out by screaming, started playing a Mantovani rendition of *Red House*. I grimaced.

"Don't you hate it when they do that? I asked."

He nodded "They do it to everything. But it's especially insulting when they do it to someone like Hendrix, guy was a genius"

"Did you ever see him live?"

"Almost at the Isle of Wight festival."

"Hey I was there! We might have walked by each other or sat together or something!"

"I'm sure I'd have noticed."

"Nice lie, " I said, " might even have fallen for it if you hadn't already mentioned missing the main act!"

" Well I didn't exactly miss Hendrix, I fell asleep, slept through the whole performance in fact."

"That's terrible,it was his last public performance."

"Thanks for reminding me."

"Well you can't expect sympathy for falling asleep!"

"I know, I know but I'd been out in the heat all day and by the time he came on I was, keep this under your hat okay, I have a reputation to protect here," he leant over then in order to whisper in my ear, the heat of his breath brushing my neck, "I was too stoned to sit upright any more and I made the mistake of lying down. I remember hearing Now ladies and gents here's the one you've all been waiting for and the next thing I knew Leonard Cohen was asking everyone to light a match."

Soon as he sat back my body missed him. The waitress came and plonked our Knickerbocker Glories on the table.

"Well at least you got to see Cohen" I said, picking up the long spoon and diving straight in to keep myself reaching over and grabbing Adrian.

"I've never told anyone before."

"I'm not surprised," I replied with a mouth full of ice cream, raspberry sauce and fruit cocktail. "but don't worry, I swear to never tell another soul."

"Promise?"and he shot me a look with his baby blues that sent tingles all the way down to my poor battered feet. I hadn't been looked at like that since, well since what seemed like forever.

"Promise." I gasped

"Last time I had one of these, "Adrian said with an amused smile, "was on the 10th December 1964."

"That's very precise," I noted, furious at myself, and more than a little miffed that my ridiculous overreaction was the cause of his amusement, I couldn't stop myself adding under my breath, "almost anal in fact." Of course as soon as I'd said it I regretted it. The trouble with me is, I can't keep my mouth and my emotions separate, whatever I feel comes straight out. My only hope was that Adrian hadn't heard me.

"The reason I remembered the date," he continued just moments later, " was that not only was it the first time I kissed Ruthy Brown, it was also my birthday. I don't think I'd call remembering your birthday anal exactly!"

"Me and my big mouth." I said shaking my head.

Dropping his spoon, Adrian leant across the table again. I backed away thinking, well I don't know what I was thinking because all thoughts disappeared soon as he caught hold of my chin and lifted it up till my mouth was just inches away from his.

"Doesn't look too big to me," he said and brushed his lips over mine, then sat back in his chair grinning. You can just imagine what that whisper of pressure did to my poor sex starved libido and I'm sure he could too. He was playing with me, had to be, why else would a gorgeous sexy doctor make a move on Dulcie Complelli?

I was hardly what you'd call a stunner even in my youth, my hair though a decent shade of auburn was always too untameable, and, there was no disputing that the nose I'd inherited from my Russian aristocratic great aunt looked better on her. Even my eyes, which I'd been told were my best feature, tended to reflect the weather, which was fine on bright sky blue days, but skies all too often tended to turn grey; and though I'd kept my body in decent shape by dragging it to the park three times a week and forcing it to run, well jog round, it had still been on this earth for 50 years and life hadn't always been kind.

Trouble was I wasn't used to dating games. All the dating I'd done, if that's what you could call it, was as a hippy and things were far simpler then. If a guy fancied you, or you fancied him, you just dragged each other off and had sex. I had no idea what to do now. I needed advice, and fast, so I forced my high heels back on, excused myself and went to the ladies to text Sue.

As I waited for my reply I kept fantasising rolling around on the floor with the doc and having mad passionate sex amongst the garlic bread and pizza crumbs. I waited till I couldn't wait any more. Any longer my knickerbocker glory would have started to melt and Adrian would be wondering what had happened to me. Sue would have to have her phone switched off, it seemed I was on my own. I decided the best way to avoid further embarrassment was to ignore the kiss, act in fact as if it had never happened.

"So" I asked when I was back at the table, "who's Ruthy Brown?"

"Ruthy Brown," Adrian replied searching my face probably for a reaction to the kiss, I deliberately rooted around in my knickerbocker glory, picked out a tinned strawberry, then made the mistake of swallowing it whole and had to force myself not gag, as it slid slowly down my throat like my first and only oyster.

"She was my first love. I'd lusted after her all through junior school but she never even noticed me. Long red hair, green eyes and a great mouth with soft pink lips. She was 15 and already pretty stacked and I was just a thirteen year old pimply faced boy. A couple of years at that age makes a hell of a difference."

" It certainly does" I agreed, thinking of all the spotty, farty, boys that used to hang around our school gates wolf whistling at Sabrina Thompson. Sabrina, who knew how to change a school uniform into a fashion statement, was 15 and already 'Sex on legs,' wouldn't even dirty her eyes on those poor hopefuls. Ah, the sweet hours Sue and I spent hating her. I'm sure we'd have probably hated Ruthy Brown too

"So how d'you get your kiss?" I asked ignoring the ridiculous pangs of jealousy, at the thought of him kissing anyone else, curdling the ice cream in my stomach.

"More of a peck really, but it was on the lips. Sammy, my best friend at the time, had not only bought me a birthday Knickerbocker Glory at the Wimpy bar where we always hung out, but poured about half a bottle of Vodka, stolen from his parents liquor cabinet, into my coke. Then he dared me to drink it. After that asking Ruthy for a birthday kiss was easy."

"And she gave you one, just like that?"

"Just like that," Adrian agreed. "Sometimes who dares wins." When he casually pushed back a lock of hair that had fallen across my face I wanted to cry. I watched his tongue come out to find an escaped crumb which had landed on his lip after he bit into the wafer, and I longed to be that crumb and be licked, sucked then swallowed.

Adrian picked up his glass, his finger accidentally,or at least I think it was accidentally, brushed against mine. I surreptitiously glanced down at my phone which was lying on my lap but there was still no message. God Sue, where are you when I need you? I could feel little Miss Desperate making an appearance. I knew from bitter experience how everyone hated her, so, I finished my wine and when Adrian poured me more I finished that as well. "Pizza always makes me thirsty," I lied "What about your first kiss?" He asked.

The wine finally hit me and I began to relax, " Guy" I answered "I always remember his name because his birthday was on Bonfire night. God knows what his parents were thinking of but Guy didn't seem bothered by kids snide remarks, he could rise above them. I think that's what first attracted me to him, that, his silky blonde hair and his tree house of course." I could still remember the light-headed freedom I'd experienced, when I'd first looked down from the tree house after Guy pulled up the rickety rope ladder we'd climbed, knowing that our parents could never climb up and stop us no matter what we got up to. "We'd climb up to the tree house with our packets of sunset yellow sherbet and experiment. One of us would eat the sherbet then we'd kiss with plenty of tongue to see how long we'd have to keep them in each other's mouth before the colour was transferred. Wasn't long before we stopped bothering with the sherbet."

I'd been so busy reminiscing I hadn't noticed that Adrian had stopped eating his Knickerbocker glory and was just sitting there with his spoon poised over what was left. His skin, I now saw, had turned sort of greenish.

"Are you okay?" I asked, "You've gone a bit green. "

Suddenly he dropped his spoon and clapping a hand over his mouth ran around the room looking for a toilet. Not finding one fast enough he rushed outside. You could hear him heaving even with the door closed, great spews of vomit spilling over the pavement. A couple of little boys left the table to lean against the plate glass window and watch, crying when their mother came to drag them away.

Of course it totally put me off the rest of my Knickerbocker Glory. I called our waitress over and explained what had happened and she called the manager. He couldn't get rid of me fast enough. He tore up our bill, put a couple of free meal tokens in my hand and almost pushed me out the door. By that time Adrian had stopped throwing up and was leaning, legs shaking, against the wall for support. I felt pretty bad knowing it was my fault we'd gone to the restaurant, but surely any fool knew not to eat seafood at a pizza joint. He didn't look green any more but he was terribly pale.

"How you feeling?" I asked and when he didn't answer added,

"Maybe you should see a doctor." He gave me this ha, ha very funny look, then mumbled that he just needed to go home and lie down.

"The manager was very apologetic," I told him and I waved the two free tokens at him, " Look he even gave me these."

Adrian just groaned so I phoned him a cab. When it came he staggered over and threw himself in. The taxi took off before I'd even had time to ask if he needed me to accompany him. He didn't even wave goodbye.

After he'd gone I just stood around for a bit feeling sorry for myself knowing that now I'd never find out if he was being serious or not. At least I'd have stood a chance if, instead of being afraid of sounding like a Jewish mother, I'd warned him about possible seafood poisoning. Well it was all too bloody late now as the possibility of a second date with a good looking doctor with a sense of humor and an almost Brad Pitt mouth was, let's face it, after such a disaster, a big fat zero.

It was still fairly early and the night air felt balmy and full of possibilities. All around me, or so it seemed, couples were out walking hand in hand. That could have been me. Knowing I'd get horribly depressed if I went home I decided to walk through the park. It was perfectly safe on warm nights like these as there were always lots of dog walkers and gangs of those new age hippy types sitting around drumming or fire juggling. A hint of a breeze carried the sweet scent of early flowers to my spring-starved nose.

I took off my shoes. The pavement felt cool and soothing. Halfway home I found the cherry tree. It was in full blossom and I stood beneath it and let the breeze do what no man had ever done, turn me into a bride, pink confetti falling down over me. I looked back after I'd walked away and the tree seemed to shimmer against the night sky and I decided that tomorrow I'd get up early and come here and spend the whole day drawing it. By the time I got home I was almost cheerful.

TIM SHELTON-JONES

Apart

I ask if the green fields care,
If the grass spreading under a slow-warming sun
Is a tender bed laid down to bring us rest,
And all the marguerites and kingcups and cow-parsley
Are looking out for passing souls, to nod them a welcome.
It feels that way.

So I wonder what it does to a heart
To grow so far from their touch,
Living with stone and steel and manufactured lights -
My heart. Your heart.

Care of the Parent

The Park is a blanket, heavy upon me
and my breath comes slowly, slumberous as warm mud.
Mother, on my arm, just laughs: some toddler
or furry creature pleases her.
Then she remembers Jerusalem - the heat. And (yet again)
the thunderstorms of Berlin, wet clothes
pressing to her skin, the rain
roaring its attack upon the city.
Joyous.

Or maybe I am driftwood
and this summer's day's a river, steaming
impolitely with life. So I must circle here
through the eddies of café, rose garden, lake,
never sucked right in, never moving on. Becalmed.
Even the clouds have scuttled far, the horizon
bare, but for a barrier of mist. A perfect circle. Other figures
tread the pretty lawns, families defined
by tweeds, or teenagers, or tie-die shirts. This is all I can see.
Pictures.
I crave the reality.

The Visit

I was there, you know
Among the shoes dusty in their aged heaps,
Wandering the corridors of blackened brick,
Trying to hear inside the emptiness.
Outside, a criss-cross of rails in the wasted grass
Made iron maps without meaning.
I was there, and came away
Seeing nothing but sunlight falling in familiar ways,
The wide fields all around still golden with wheat.
For history lives elsewhere
In voices,
Those who are left to speak.
And I am there too, you know,
Amongst all those words
As they fall, each day,
An everlasting rain.

The Passing of Time

I've no time to think
no time to cry
no time to ask
no time to reply
no time to give way
no time to drop by
no time to stop
and no time to die.
There's no time
For time anymore
Not even just
to say
Goodbye.

String Theory

Armed with my little knowledge, my dangerous thing,
I seek to unravel the secrets of time.
But will I be able to ravel them back again
Or will we be left in a mess of string ?

Raw

Break me open
I am an egg,
Brittle on the outside
My shell thin as thinking,
But inside
I am all goo,
A soft organic sea -
Transparent home
To a plump squishy sphere of hope.
Probe my golden globe gently
And I yield.
But prick or stab
And I am undone,
An unbounded river
Palely spreading.
I will find you and cling
To your clothes, your heart
Your skin. Ergo
This fragile carapace,
This dry, silent entreaty
To know and yet respect
My secret deliciousness.
But if you do not break me
I must burst with my own goodness
Devouring my own heart
To become purblind enquiry,
And a pitiful thin crying
All dressed softly in the sunlight
Of my bold new feathers.

Computer Rage

The waste of time
The fear of disaster
The toxic light, its unblinking square
Of pitiless information.
"You are recommended to back up before continuing"
- but I can't find reverse.
This is hard as a gravel road,
Riding pillion, ninety miles an hour,
And I'm clinging to a one-speed half-brain
With all of hell's hackers burning the highway towards us.
The crash when it comes
Could be very messy, bits everywhere.
A hard drive indeed.

Everyone's least favourite Bird

Nobody could call you graceful.
Even in flight you flap noisily
Your fat ball of a body cannoning its way through the atmosphere
A poo-bomb, ready to explode.
Every building is fortified against you,
Spiked and sealed. Signs decorate our public places
"Do not feed the pigeons". Rats on wings
They say, and screaming infants persecute you
So brave beneath those proud parental smiles.
Yet, as sunlight fires your iridescent cloak,
Pinks wink and greys play hide-and-seek upon you
And your neckerchief of white or black bobs jaunty as you walk.

Ah, you suffer this contempt
Because you're common (yet no two of you the same!).
If only you were rare! How those twitchers would flock
To marvel at your comic dignity. Whole woodlands would be fenced -
A Garden of Eden, just for you,
Your small-town strut fed secretly to the Nation's screens
While wide-eyed Attenboroughs and Oddies whispered their delight
At your muted warble - that submarine clarinet
Of a voice. But no. As it is
It's left to soft old girls
To scatter crumbs for you around the benches
Of our parks and gardens, risking arrest
For hazarding the public health. Because
As well you know
You're really just another
Common-or-garden
Misbegotten
Familiarity-breeds-contempt
Pest.

Storm Lover

I am in love with you, storm,
Your pounding fist
Of a heart,
Your creature roar
Your open-mouthed appetite for everything around.
Spitting hail, your belly
Scrapes earth clean,
Your shaggy clouds,
Hang down like entrails
Or a coarse old coat of hair
Just asking to be touched.
And I'd love to probe those lightning eyes of yours -
Have you a soul
For me to find and share? Or is your anger
The lashing of a formless Frankenstein,
A crazed half-knowing
Of your own too brief,
Too terrible
Mortality?
I ride you today
As others ride their fairground switchbacks,
Their late-night brawls
Or the storms of history -
To know life, not through smiles or pleasantries
But through extremes.
To stand on a hard-won ground,
The cruel frontier of existence
And peer out into the swirling night.
For there is no quiet end
Only the one storm
That consumes us all.

NOREEN BROWN

From Shadows Before

After six weeks absence, David had arrived late the previous night. Their love making had been fast and urgent. This suited Stella. No time for talking.

Next morning they took the children to school which surprised and pleased them. They usually made their own way. As an excuse not to be alone with him she insisted they needed to stock up. On the way home he bought her an overlarge elaborate bunch of roses.

But by now she was feeling jumpy and irritable.

She remembered moving pots; adjusting the heat, disentangling herself from David's roving hands, turning to face him. As always his dark rather sinister looks made her want to smile. The intensity of his ironic gaze.. Though his thick hair was thinning and there was a slight thickening around his waist, she still felt lucky to have found him.

"David I'm sorry but I - I have some news, something to tell you. I.." She hesitated. God! How could she have been so stupid?

She watched him carefully. His response was crucial.

"I didn't mention this before because I hoped it wasn't true. But the thing is - I'm six weeks pregnant". His voice careful, neutral he said "Pregnant? But how? I mean what about the pills. What happened? Didn't you take them?"

Angry, she turned back to the stove, switched the oven full on. Put the meat in.

"Actually yes, that's exactly what happened. You being away so long I thought I'd give myself a break. And then you came home unexpectedly and I didn't use the cap. I thought I'd get away with it."

She sighed. "We'll talk about it later. I can hear the kids arguing. Let's eat."

David reached out, pulled her close, but it was a desperate, restrained kind of hug.

"Six weeks," He patted her absently "It's not really set in stone is it?" He nibbled at her ear.

She jerked away. "Set in stone? Babies are not stones!" She could hear her voice rising. "You mean get rid of it.. Have it ab.. aborted!" The word stuck in her throat. She took a deep breath, tried to calm down.

"I can't. I just couldn't do that," she said vehemently.

"Millions of women do," he said mildly.

"Millions of women do," she mimicked tightly. "Not millions of men. God you make me sick. YOU try it. Lie on the bed, open wide, just a little discomfort. Oh I've heard all about it. You'll bleed a bit. And your breasts may be sore for a while but not to worry its all flushed away now."

She glared at his stricken face, tried to think of more to shock him but he turned away, plonked himself down at the kitchen table.

The acrid smell of burning meat filled her nostrils. That smell! She was back in the kitchen in Leitrim, aged sixteen, telling her parents she was pregnant with Grania, her illegitmate daughter,

David stood up, reached behind her, switched on the extractor fan, and smiled apologetically

But the bitter truth was, it was her own fault. He had always left that side of things to her..

Once she had overheard him argue with his Mother. Her voice tight with disapproval she'd announced, "She'll breed like an Irish peasant." But Stella's flash of anger had been assuaged by his robust reply.

"We'll come to that bridge if necessary Mother. And there is such a thing as birth control these days."

He had laughed good-naturedly.

"Anyway Stella is far from being a peasant, as you well know."

However, now pregnant for the fourth time, she conceded his mother had a point.

And looking back she knew exactly when it had happened.

The day he returned from Saudi Arabia, both of them high on each others career successes.

She, at last acknowledged as a therapist, he now head of his department, travel unlimited.

Between his longer trips away, and against good practice, she usually rested from pill taking. But this time he had returned unexpectedly, as a surprise for her birthday.

So wined and dined and hungry for each other, it was all over before she had time for the old fashioned cap she kept in reserve. She'd just hoped she'd be lucky.

"Mummy, James is cheating again. Daddy tell him," Madeline's blue eyes sparked angrily.

David laughed.

"Come on you two; let's set the table. He cheats because you're quicker than he is at word games."

With a wink at James he said. "But he's better than you at ball games. So it evens out."

Later, the children finally in bed David sat facing Stella.

He smiled hopefully.

"Is it really the end of the world? Having another child". He moved to the settee, lifted her legs down, snuggled in, and kissed the side of her mouth. "The kids would love it, you know. And so would I," he added quickly.

"Ok" she said lightly, "You have it. You stay at home give up your ego trips, top and tail an infant for the next two or three years. Lose brain cells from lack of use." She moved away, stood up, went to the kitchen found the hidden packet. Cigarette smoke whirled toward the still humming extractor.

She switched it off went back to the living room.

Sorry David. But It's all such a mess. Of course it's not the end of the world but I've just started a career. Arranged after care for the kids, began to feel like a real person again."

"Come on Stella since when were you less than real. These last few years you've been brilliant. All that studying, your degree and now this appointment."

He leaned forward. "Whatever decision you make I am right behind you. I know how you've worked for this job. Looked after the kids, looked after.." He opened his hands, gestured around - everything."

But then his eyes hardened. "But remember if you decide to go through with it I can only be there for you when I can."

This was honest enough! It was the nature of his job.

"And I agree a baby now means putting your career on hold. For at least - a year - or maybe a bit more! We can afford help - so - but I.." He stopped, aware he was floundering.

Irritably Stella lit another cigarette but after a few puffs she stubbed it out. Instead of relaxing it had made her nauseous. She crushed the half full package and threw it into the waste basket.

She couldn't, she wouldn't go through with it all again. Waddling ungainly for months, reliving her first pregnancy, struggling to love a child that wasn't Grania.

All the old guilt's resurrected.

It was after midnight before he joined her in the bedroom. She was used to his late night overseas calls. At first she'd wondered if it was a woman but then realised apart from her and the children the business was his life. The cut and thrust of new markets opening up. The hype of jetting off to wherever.

For an hour, lying flat with the duvet up to her chin she had struggled with her options.

She listened to him shower. The rapid splish spilsh of the toothbrush, his noisy gargling the, familiar homely sounds which were part of their marriage.

He came into the bedroom, stood towelling his hair smiling at her between the rubbings. He threw the towel onto a chair. Sat on the side of he bed.

"David. I think I've decided". She took a deep breath. "I just can't go through…" she hesitated. She could still change her mind.

Naked, he climbed beneath the sheet. She could feel his body heat. The old familiar conflicts rising. The urge to enfold, to protect him from his male vulnerabilities, to have him hold and protect her and like sexless beings just drift to childlike sleep. She often thought that was all she needed. She could do without the rest.

But he was experienced, had taught her, slowly and intensely how to let go, to journey with him. She had been a willing and apt pupil.

She knew that with a lesser lover, she would never have known such transports of delight.

However as a tutor he had made a rod for his own back and now was enslaved by his pupil

She sat up, aware of her power. For all his high profile success, and his arrogant good looks it only took a hint of sexual rejection to topple him.

He looked at her enquiringly, waited.

She took a deep breath.

"I've decided! I'll see Paul soon as I can get an appointment". She looked away. "And if he won't help I know someone who knows someone".

"You mean abortion?" He stared at her, his gaze unreadable.

He scratched his earlobe, a sure sign of disapproval. "Well I suppose if that's what you have decided…"

Their G.P .Paul Lewes was an old Rugby friend.

His arm around her waist, his hand fondling her right breast he said, "Would you like me to have a word with him?"

Her left breast felt rejected.

Right now he would have a word with the Pope if it pleased her. She never ceased to be awed by the speed of his erection

"No," she said, "Its my decision. I'll deal with it."

Their love making after all was a flop. Stella just couldn't respond.

They turned away from each other.

"Sorry" she murmured. "Not to worry," he said. "Got a lot on your mind."

He slid out of bed. The shower splashed loud, full force.

Angry she turned away. Her face in the pillow. This bloody house! The bathroom, too close! Every sound! They'd agreed the place was too small.

He'd promised they would upmarket but it didn't really worry him. Away such a lot...

Next morning eyes averted, treading carefully around the burning issue, they decided to keep the children away from school and had a real beach. They walked to the end of the pier, and David took the children on everything that moved.

They ate in a glass enclosed restaurant facing the sea. The place was lively with a few parents and children amongst the usual cliental.

At the next table a young mother discretely breast fed her baby. Stella could see the tiny puckered face, hear the strong sucking sounds and for an incredible moment felt a small tug at her own breasts and thought Grania! It was the dark hair on the minuscule head... Black! Like Granias! And Rory's. How proud he would have been of Grania! Confused she watched the tiny fingers clutching and kneading. She looked away, closed her mind but the damage had been done. How could she even think of it. How live with herself afterwards. Why add guilt to the many.

Aware David was watching her she met his eyes across the table.. For a second everything faded. There was just the two of them. He smiled slightly, shrugged one shoulder, shook his head from side to side.

She felt a huge sense of release.

She looked back at the baby, the mother's slim hand now gently caressing the tiny head.

For whatever reason, she decided, there would be no abortion.

ALANNA MCINTYRE

Synchronicity

Avocado stones in dark earth,
regularly watered, buried unseen
swollen germination, shoot leaves,
unexpected joyous breakthrough.

Unseen treasures revealed by
incoming tides, flotsam and
jetsam, reworked as fingers
weave, plait, and knot,
with coloured strands,
given up by the sea,
through washed up fishing net.
Mind enthralled by gifts from
waves, art is nurtured by
unexpected finds.

Introduced to Sarah Jane,
a herbalist, by my daughter
Gemma. We all love nature.
Arrange to meet at a nearby
allotment to harvest
restorative golden rod.
Explore the vegetation together.
Nature is symbiotic, nettle and
Dock grows side by side.

All thee things happen
within a week,
signs of life re-rooting.

The Allotment

The allotment is paradise, a world on its own.
Hops and vines straddle on the back fence,
fledgling box hedges pattern the edges.
Nasturtiums sprawl colourful neckties
around, leeks, marrows, onions and beets.
Sunflowers stand tall and survey the scene,
while beans shoot forth scarlet flowers,
heralding the late runners to come.
Caterpillars invade cabbages, leaving
love hole marks.
Planning and precision with every spade dug.
couch weed pulled, paths carpeted,
and laid pallets of wood construct the beds.
Incandescent butterfly wings reverberate
threads of colour of flowering chive, purple leaf,
and orange tagetes, pest protection,
planted between tomatoes.
Fruit bushes, herbs, flowers and veg
are nurtured into being.
Precious stolen hours of freedom,
away from caring for others.

Captivate the Joy

It looked like a cd
hanging from the tree.
On closer inspection
a perfectly formed spider's
web, sun gilded silver,
a rainbow spectrum,
dangled in the breeze.
I thought I had my camera,
but not today, so I jotted
this down to captivate the joy.

Jam Sandwich

Bread and butter routine,
life slapped into place
automatic pilot on,
work, iron, wash, feed,
perfunctory clean;
phrases float to mind
gelled on paper to
fruit later on,
in a jam sandwich.

Clouds

Clouds engulf the sky in a white
cameo of etched grey, soon
azure slivers of sky spread
like watercolour on wet paper.
The sky palate changes as the
breeze teases colour changes
and transforms the
cloudscape
minute by minute.

Falling

Slippered nights, creep up
on daylight hours.
Deciduous decay hangs
windswept and damp until,
vermillion, jettisons yellow,
ochre and burnt sienna
in a last onslaught before
mottled paper colours
spiral down to be crushed
underfoot.

Rose

The rose is a stately bloom
pearl pink petals splay out,
while the central bud is curled
waiting for warmth to unfurl.
The smell is citrus fresh
with the clarity of youth
and the purity of a pink
streaked dawn sky.

Honeysuckle

Honeysuckle smells warm and sweet
you want to smell it again and again.
There is comfort in the familiarity.
The flowerets wear scalloped party
dresses and the stamens offer
a filigree of golden opportunity.

Hyacinths

The sweetness wafts as you
bend down to admire the
bright blue colour. It makes
you want to breathe in deeply
to capture the heady fragrance.

Magnolia Flower

A magnolia flower
is a waxen light
on a candlelabra of green.
It gives off a fragrance
of the East and opens like
an opulent jewel
withstanding wind and rain.

Chanting

Chanting helps clear the fear.
It stills the mind in the present,
washes worries away.
The repetition energises the system,
different rhythms emphasise
different words, butterflies in
the stomach disappear,
and the way forward is clear.

Waves of Memory

Waves of memory
lost in a sea
of seizures,
fragments surface
now and again
from deep blue depths,
others sink under
tidal waves,
lost treasure
hidden forever.

Your mind buzzes with
ideas, sparked
sherbet fireworks in the sky.
Their magical patterns
momentarily captured by night.
You scribble furiously
to describe the exploding
thoughts before they flee.
Another strand of light
invades and distracts
your racing mind.

Friendship

Friends are the people,
who are the most important.
The warp and weft of life,
links in the daisy chain.
Making daisy chains,
childhood pastime,
long stemmed flowers,
specially picked,
and interwoven to be used,
as a necklace or tiara,
so fragile and beautiful.
Flowers will fade,
friends free
your inner child.

Seizure

Your eyes glaze, you become pale,
muscles no longer hold their shape.
You fall to the ground,
your mouth twitches,
your throat gurgles,
and swallowing sounds
echo.
As your limbs stiffen
and relax in turn,
your breathing is resonant
and laboured you snore.
As your seizure stops
gradually the body slumps
into a state of peace.
You sleep,
I check your airway.
The past days depression will lift
your body has exorcised
its pent up electricity.

TANYA MURRAY

Lamia, dressed in all of Mary

When from this wreathed tomb shall I awake!
When move in a sweet body fit for life,
And love, and pleasure, and the ruddy strife
Of hearts and lips!
John Keats, Lamia, Part 1

This is how it started:

"Oh, and I fixed that squeaky hinge on the bathroom door. And, er, well..."

He forced a grin, glanced at his watch, hated himself. The betrayal in that small gesture. (Did she notice? Could she? If she didn't, did it matter?) Two minutes before Visiting was over. Two minutes. How could that seem so long?

"Well, hon? Now you say something, remember?"

Making a poor joke of it, like they used to. After the diagnosis. Before it got bad.

The thing of it was: Mary was still Mary. Still beautiful.

Oh God, so beautiful.

Same fine-boned face. Same sea green eyes. Only - not the same.

She sat with hands clasped neatly, in this Visiting Room, in The Home. A room painted in bright cheerful colours. Fresh cut flowers in a vase by the window. Sweeping views across the well maintained lawns, to smoky autumnal hills beyond. Smartly uniformed staff whispered about, smiling, kind. It was a beautiful place. A very expensive place, more than he could afford, actually. The Home, yes. But not her home. It could never be that.

Polite, quizzical, she waited; a faint smile on her perfect lips, (...Lips I kissed, and mouth explored and hands touched and bodies touched and joined and thought would never end...)

She looked at him. Or rather, in his direction. Did she see him? The eyes now. Still sea green. Eyes, once, to swim in. Only... Not swimming now. Drowning. The sea, clouded. And a storm of night terrors coming, perhaps. Or worse, much worse, a few minutes, a few hours, of something like lucidity. The cruellest. To know what was lost. But no, don't even think of that...

The bell rang. Thank God for the bell. He kissed her again, slow, on the forehead so she wouldn't see his tears. Not that it mattered. To her, at least. 'Sometimes', his therapist had said 'you just need to feel that wetness on your cheeks.'

"Sweet cheeks," she said. He forced it all back in, behind a smile.

"Yes, hon?"

"Can you do something about that squeaky hinge in the bathroom? It's driving me nuts."

The smile trembled on his drawn face.

"Sure hon. I'll get right on it."

She winced slightly, and he realised how hard he was squeezing her pale hand.

"Right on it, I promise."

That night he sat on the bed they had shared, in the house they had loved, and held the nightdress he bought her two Christmases ago (only two?), and buried his face in it, and drank in the smell of her, still fresh, still there, carefully trapped in the polythene hanger bags he had put over all of her clothes, the first weekend she went to The Home.

Just for respite care, they'd said. Everyone knowing that wasn't true.

Her clothes. Just: keeping them for her, for when she needed them again. And now, her wardrobe was full of polythene shrouds.

He buried his face in the flimsy fabric of the nightdress and took a great, gulping breath. Her perfume, sweet and delicate, and young, enveloped him; and he raged.

Young, yes. Too young for this. 'Early-onset', they called it. 'Very rare.' Not rare enough. Who the hell gets Alzheimers at forty?

This wasn't the contract he made with life. They were supposed to get old and cranky together, and live a long, long time. The contract stank. There had to be a get out clause.

There was.

He used his contacts at the University. Spoke vaguely of a research proposal. One outside his usual field. Something new, he said, radical, cross-cultural. Some nonsense about informing oil field geophysics with indigenous geomantic knowledge. Trying, hard to hide his desperation. Because this was surely desperate. If not insane.

Which is how he found himself, late one damp October afternoon in the book-choked study of a professor of Comparative Epistomologies, on the far side of the campus from his own neat, modern cubicle in the Earth Sciences Department.

Aptly enough, the professor seemed intent on taking a geological era fussing with a pipe, tamping tobacco into the bowl, sucking wetly on the stem, dropping dead match after dead match into an overflowing ashtray, beneath an institutional notice Thanking you for Not Smoking on College Premises.

He wanted to hit this absurd man, to punch and smash at him. Didn't he realise? They were wasting time. He was wasting time. And she had so little of it left.

He forced his fists to unclench, focussing on the wan sodium gleam of a lampost outside the window, waging it's own lonely war with the growing dark.

"What do you...mm... know of... the Lamia, Richard?"

The professor spoke at last, had finally sucked life from the foul-smelling, clotted mass of tobacco. He punctuated his words with smug little puffs of smoke. Richard hated him; forced an interested smile.

"I don't know," he said. "The same as anyone, I suppose. Wasn't it a poem by Byron? Some kind of mythical creature? Half woman, half serpent?"

The professor smiled back, let out another self-congratulatory puff; teasing him, making him wait for it. This must be how he was with his students. An old fraud, in a third rate provincial university, hoarding his little scraps of knowledge.

"Keats, actually. Predictably, perhaps, a rather – romantic – take on an old legend. A very old legend... And much nastier than Keats would have you believe. She was a mother who killed her children, you see. Worse than that. Devoured them, actually. The Ancient Greeks formulated it of course, incorporated it into their own pantheon. That colourful knack they had for the apt punishment..."

His gaze drifted upward, his voice acquiring a high, hectoring tone. He was lecturing, now.

"...Cursed never to close her eyes, you see, so she could never avoid, constantly, witnessing the awfulness of the thing she did... In some readings, she can actually remove her unblinking eyes, and hold them in her hands... In this telling, she became a kind of child-stealing wicked witch archetype, bled into allied myths like Hansel & Gretel, the Russian Baba Yar; a story to frighten small Greek children with, even now... In others, she became a kind of embodiment of female original sin, a Lillith figure... the serpent imagery obvious here, of course, vagina dentata, the devouring woman, this being the path that Keats chose to deviate from so picturesquely... but I believe there is yet an older myth, at least pre-Assyrian, that all these are only echoes of, a secret within a secret, an Ur-text, if you will..."

"Why... Are... You... telling me... this?"

Perhaps the professor caught the suppressed rage. He halted, mid flow. Frowned. Looked steadily at Richard for a long moment, then set the pipe aside, and scribbled on a Post It note. The lecture was spoilt. Or – perhaps – the intense, anguished man opposite had, in some obscure way... scared him.

"I'm not entirely sure I understand what it is you say you are researching, Richard. And I'm not sure I want to know. But if you are set on this course, then go and see this man. He may be able to help."

Richard looked at the scrap of yellow paper in his hand. A mobile phone number. And a single name.

Rackham.

After Richard had left, after he had sucked life back into his pipe, the old fraud sat for a long time in the growing darkness. A thin wind-lashed rain had begun to fall, making a sound like handfuls of gravel thrown against the glass of the study window. He shuddered.

"And may God help you,", he muttered, to the indifferent heavens.

Now Richard was in another room, meeting another man. Tall, lean, entirely bald. Age: impossible to guess. A neatly trimmed horseshoe mustache. The blackest, deepest-set eyes. Something monkish about him. A stillness, a watchful, knowing patience, nothing - unnecessary. But when he moved, rising silently from a wingbacked armchair in this quiet, private room, in this exclusive members club, he moved like a dancer, or a boxer: economical, graceful. Purposeful.

His handshake was dry and confident. Strength there, but no need to show it. He wore a single silver hoop earring, more silver over the grey silk of his shirt, at his wrists, on his fingers. Trashy Hells Angel bling at odds with the understated quality of his perfectly cut black business suit. A successful night club owner? Retired drug dealer? Lawyer for a biker gang perhaps? Richard had Googled him ahead of the meeting. Nothing came up. Nothing at all.

Rackham.

In fact, according to the professor, he was some kind of maverick anthropologist, beyond the academic pale. Off the grid, off the map. Off all the maps. Years spent in the Earth's dark corners. Learning rituals.

It had cost five hundred pounds just to be in this room with him. Ten thousand pounds more, if he did what he said he could. Richard had it in twenty four hours. The car, the last of his small inheritance put by to finance the care home. None of it mattered. All gambled on this last roll of the dice.

Oddly, when he handed the money over, the most cash Richard had ever handled in his life, Rackham didn't even glance at the fat brick of fifties, just tossed it onto the chair behind him uncounted. As if the money were simply a test of something. Of seriousness. Intent.

"You realise Mr...?"

Richard swallowed nervously. He remembered the last thing the professor had said to him.

'Be careful, Richard. Rackham is dangerous.'

"Call me Smith. It's as good a name as any."

"Of course. Smith. This is only a... finders fee. I am a mere agent. The final - much larger - payment is made... elsewhere."

"I understand."

"I wonder if you really do, hmmm? But your mind is made up, and I have your money. So: a bargain is a bargain, and we have shaken on it. And with that..."

He made a curious, theatrical gesture with his left hand, as if plucking a dandelion clock and blowing its' seeds away:

"...It is done. I will leave you now. You will not reach me on that telephone number again. But – just one question. What did the professor tell you a lamia was?"

"A... demon?"

Rackham laughed.

"Did he now? No, Mr.Smith. The professor has only half of it. She is not merely a demon. Much more interesting than that. She is... Something else entirely."

It was a miracle, they said. Spontaneous remission. Unheard of. Maybe there'd been a misdiagnosis... Perhaps some more tests? There might be a relapse...

He didn't care. He took Mary home. Candles, dinner, wine. And talk. Endless talk. The luxury of it, after interminable months of silence. He tested her at first, and she was amused, and teased him, but she got every single one right: the title of that movie, ruined by a woman in the audience giving birth in the middle of it back when they first met. The nickname they gave their first car... Soon, he gave up testing. Just talked. Listened. Laughed. Really laughed, for the first time since the diagnosis.

They kissed again, like they used to, her hunger answering his. (Her hunger. Greater than his.)

One more test. He was nervous. He had to know.

"Mary... Are - you - really back?"

She smiled and pressed a finger to his lips.

"Wait there."

She called him into the bedroom a few minutes later. She was on the bed. In the nightdress. Gorgeous.

They made love. And it was like it was when they were young. Slow and soft, tender, and timeless. But it had to end, and at the end there was a terrible sweet pain and he felt something tear loose inside, a part of him he didn't even know he had, and it whirled away and was gone and he knew it would always be like this now, one piece then another until one day there would be nothing left, and he would be done, the final payment made. But it didn't matter. If only...

"Mary, it really is you, isn't it?"

She smiled. Her green eyes. Unclouded.

"You brought me back. Your love brought me back and I'm here and I'll always be here for you. That is our contract. Till death, sweet cheeks. Remember?"

"Till death? Is that all?"

He laughed, and then he cried.

"I remember."

She held him till the sobs faded, and he slept, so he never heard the lamia cry too, alone in the dark.

Not for the lie she told, because demons trade in lies; and besides Mary's every thought and dream and hope were in her, and she was in Mary, and so who could say she wasn't Mary?

Nor for the theft of his soul by inches, because demons are long lived but mortal too and must do what they do to survive. No, she cried because of the price she paid in the contract.

Because she had dared to yearn, to feel wind in her hair; to taste chocolate, swim in the sea, laugh, hear a gull cry... and to feel a man inside her, especially that, it was her nature...

To be human, for just a short while, she had, as she must, dressed herself in all of Mary.

So she knew each bittersweet day that she loved him with Mary's love, she damned him a little more. And he, the poor fool, not knowing, as she did, what truly awaited him on the other side, thought a few more fleeting human years of happiness worth that awful price.

She stared unblinking into the darkness that embraced them both, rocked him and wept; loved, and hungered for him, her man-child, and considered:

Maybe it was.

Undying

Rackham was dead. He had been dead, he guessed, for about five minutes now. Ten, since the thick walls of the alembic exploded, turning the heavy conical flask into a grenade of copper shrapnel and scalding fluid.

A slow count to six hundred comprising: five undignified minutes spent in the actual chore of dying, thrashing and jerking, gasping and shivering as he bled out from a severed femoral artery; and the five minutes since then, spent being just, well… dead.

He marvelled at his composure, in view of the circumstances. Composure, not stillness. The stillness came easy now. In fact, it really didn't require any effort at all.

Fragments from the blast must have done something to his spine, he supposed, because in the immediate aftermath - ten minutes, a life time ago - after the white-out blindness had ebbed, and the ringing in his ears subsided to the merely intolerable, as his battered brain slowly pieced together the surprising news that he was not in fact, dead already, but merely dying… That was when he realised he could feel nothing below the waist.

He had awoken slumped like a discarded rag doll in one corner of the cellar, opposite the stairs, wedged behind the still-intact half of the heavy oak lab bench.

The overhead lights had been taken out in the blast, but enough October morning sunlight filtered through the storm windows for him to surmise that the rapidly growing shiny patch of slickness in which he lay was his own blood.

He had wasted some of his five minutes' dying attempting, with spastic imprecision from his pinned semi prone position beneath the bench, to guide his fist into the ragged hole in his numb groin, to stem the painless warm oily spurting his fingers felt there. Useless, of course.

Soon, the numbness below his waist was echoed by a different, colder numbness above.

He found he was panting for breath. The edges of his vision grew fuzzy, colours leaching away. His arms felt clumsy. Too heavy to lift. He was tired now. He let his arms sink to the floor, felt the cooling stickiness of his own blood on the back of his hands. He sighed.

No point in calling out. No one would come. It was why he had bought this place, the failed farmstead deep in the back woods. Somewhere quiet, a long way from neighbours, where he could play with dead things, undisturbed.

Finding the old graveyard had been a bonus; finding The Book in the last grave he robbed... Well, that had been the clincher. It was almost as if it had been meant to be.

If he had been a religious man, he might have offered up a prayer of thanks then. After so many years of searching, to just have the answer land in his lap like that...

But Rackham prayed to no Gods, known or unknown. He wasn't even superstitious. An impartial observer might consider this strange, given his particular interests. Yet he considered himself a true student of natural philosophy, a scientist. Others disagreed. They called him different names:

Satanist. Sorcerer. Madman.

This was because they saw only what he had done, sometimes to people they cared about. They did not know why he had done them.

That his chosen field was labelled 'magic' by the ignorant was their problem, not his. If pressed to name it himself, he would simply call it, accurately, the Occult. As in hidden. No more, no less.

After all, there had been a time when magic and science were one natural philosophy, when Dr. John Dee, the foremost applied mathematician of his age, could turn from his navigational calculations for the British Navy to read the future in a Mayan scrying stone; and Francis Bacon could argue for technocracy while trying to turn lead into gold. Science and magic, two sides of the same coin.

Only relatively recently in the span of human time had Science arrogantly claimed for itself dominion over all.

But one did not have to believe in Gods or Demons to realise that there were energies in the Universe as yet unexplained by science, and maybe rules for working with them too. Consider, for instance, the life force, what the ancient Sanskrit texts called 'vril'.

Rackham had.

From the time of his first murder, he was fascinated by it. What was it that - passed - at the moment of death, transforming the animate to mere meat? It was clear it was not simply a matter of electricity. The tiny, measurable charges in every living cell were sign, not signifier. As the rotting began, chemical and electrical reactions still occurred, and life - many forms of life, in fact - went on, even in dead flesh. Only the organising principal was lost.

And if this organising principal - this Vril, Chi, Reiki, Orgone energy, it had many names - could be isolated…? Well then, it might be possible to live a very long time indeed. Perhaps, forever.

So he had approached this idea, as he approached all other things: rationally, objectively. He had certain strengths in addressing the problem. He knew that he was not like other people in many ways, some useful, some… potentially problematic. Legally speaking.

'Psychopath'- that was another name he had been called.

He knew that one of the reasons they called him that, one of the chief ways he - differed - was that he really, truly, did not fear anything. Not that he was reckless. Far from it. Everything Rackham did, he did carefully. After all, it would not do for the sheep to see the wolf amongst them. But it did mean that he had no fear of death. In truth, death itself merely bored him.

Rackham on the other hand was intensely interested in Rackham, and, it followed from this, in Rackham's continued existence.

And so, some years ago, with typical care and planning Rackham the wolf had gone amongst the flock, to cemeteries and to nurseries, and his experiments in life and death had begun.

Nothing worked.

An ordinary man would have given up in frustration.

But Rackham, no ordinary man, taking time out from his studies here and there to collect a pay check from this gang boss or that jilted wife, merely for doing what he enjoyed most anyway, applied his formidable intellect to another aspect of the problem, and kept on at it.

He studied the Key of Solomon, became expert on the hidden meanings within all the Houses of the Sephiroth, read the Tibetan Book of the Dead in the original Brahmi script; even acquired one of the three authenticated Papyri of Ani, the Egyptian Hymn to Osiris.

The Books of Shadows, the magickal diaries, the library of Grimoire he assembled would have been the envy of any occultist, had they known of it.

He became adept at many things, and proved to his own satisfaction that certain conjunctions of words and symbols, mental states and objects could indeed channel and direct energies unknown to Science.

Some of these arts made his paid freelance activities immeasurably easier. Then there came a time when he could, if he had wished it, have achieved great earthly riches and power. But to what end?

The nagging thought of there one day being a world without Rackham in it drove Rackham on… There was a story he told himself when distraction beckoned too ardently.

Once, he had been hired to meet a young gambler. The man, being not fearless, only reckless, had bluffed his way to a fortune. He should have quit then, but didn't.

Things changed. The young mans' debts had grown as fast as his luck had run out. Faster. Then Rackham happened to him.

Afterwards, dropping body parts and chum off the back of a game fishing boat, two miles out from Key West, Rackham had wiped the blood off the thick end of an arm to read the tattoo on the young man's bicep.

A black and a red heart, and a scroll beneath. "Live forever or die in the attempt," it said.

Rackham grinned. Rare for him.

"Half right."

The arm followed the rest of the young man into the boat's pink wake.

Unlike the gambler, Rackham didn't do anything by halves.

But now?

Now, Rackham was still dead in the cellar, and still, despite this significant impediment, thinking.

His head, in the final agony, had come to rest on his chest, eyes open. The posture gave him a fixed view of the lower half of his body and a patch of cellar floor.

He had wondered briefly if he, the great expert of death, witness to the passing of so many others, had misread the signs.

Was this merely paralysis, the damage below the waist spreading above? But no. There was no rise and fall in his chest. Stillness in his heart. No movement anywhere. At least, not from him.

The first flies had arrived almost as his last twitches subsided, drawn at first to the heady smells of fresh blood and torn flesh in his groin. The egg laying began almost immediately. His eyes, the soft parts of his nostrils, and mouth were next.

The patch of light from the cellar window tracked across the floor, faded, returned. He lost count how often.

It was the alembic of course. Or rather, its' contents. A dreadful irony, after all the years of seeking.

Rackham pondered coolly: if the text of the graveyard book had been correct; if the process had finished correctly; if he had lived to drink the distillate: who, or what might he be now?

The distillate.

He must have ingested some of it, albeit in a somewhat unorthodox fashion, punched into his guts along with shards of shattered copper, killing him and saving him all at once.

An unmeasured, incomplete dose. How long could it last?

He found himself wondering if there would be any side effects. Realised the absurdity of that.

Time passed.

The processes of corruption ran their course. Adipocere turned body fat to foetid margarine as hydrogen released from his decaying bowel bubbled through his tissues.

His corpse broke wind, his gut swelled like an expectant mothers', and burst. The maggots itched abominably; hatched; fed; and flew away. Then the rats came.

The scientist in him noted things. In this death, there was no sleep. No release in dreams. Just an agonising wait every night, listening to the rats feed.

Below the waist he still felt nothing. Above? A symphony of pain, as filthy, squealing animals tore at him.

A normal man would have sought refuge in insanity then, and Rackham tried. But, perhaps because he was not normal, this option was denied him.

Roughly one week into his afterlife, another odd fact emerged.

Both eyes, so delicate, so soft, had gone quickly, of course, colonised by the flies, drawn out in jellied shreds by the rats, the fluid within trickling like thick salty tears down the ruined muscle and stripped flesh of his cheeks, and for a while there had been only darkness.

But now his vision had come back.

Slowly at first, a mere greying of the dark over many days and nights. It was okay. He was growing used to waiting. And Rackham permitted himself an unfamiliar emotion: hope.

Perhaps he had after all ingested enough of the stuff. To somehow - regenerate, albeit slowly.

But then his newly restored vision, fixed as before, cleared and showed him with pin-sharp clarity the progression of the decay in his lower body, and he knew. There would be no resurrection.

Judging by the track of sun and shade across the cellar floor, it took something like a year, he guessed, for his body to become completely skeletonised.

Along the way, the bacterial and animal activity precipitated some changes of viewpoint.

For about a month his head had hung back off his shoulders, and he had stared at a four by four foot square of low cellar ceiling. It was spectacularly uninteresting.

Then, the loss of flesh from his abdomen and some random rat jostlings brought his skull pitching forward again, to more or less the same position as before. Well, at least it had been a change of scene.

Gradually the animal visits tailed off; ceased. There was nothing left to eat. Rackham knew that his brain had gone. That is to say, the organ within his skull was no more. His mind remained un-dimmed. A puzzle for philosophers.

He had spent some time - some great, immeasurable amount of time, it being the one commodity he was infinitely rich in now - hoping to detect some sign that the distillate was, if not restoring him, then at least slackening its' grip, that he might at least look forward to a future, no matter how distant, when he could slide at last into the blissful peace of oblivion. But there was no such sign.

Had he been a believer, he might have considered himself damned. But Rackham did not believe.

More time passed.

One morning, or afternoon, maybe a year, maybe a decade later, a new thought occurred to him. A metaphysical experiment.

It went against everything he felt to be true, and Rackham sensed in some terrible, final way that it marked the beginning of an awful decline to ultimate humiliation. But at least it was something new to think about.

He concentrated on the mental picture of the necessary words, steeling himself.

Two rats sat squabbling on the skeletons' shoulders. One lunged at the other. It skittered for the high ground of Rackhams' skull, jumped on it, then squealed in alarm, scurrying back as the skull pitched backward off the spinal column, bouncing and rolling onto the dusty cellar floor.

For an instant, the cartwheeling view brought a lurch of remembered nausea to Rackams' mind. His world was now inverted, his skull rocking on its' crown close by the cellar steps. He fought for focus. The words formed.

"Okay. Enough. I repent. All the murders, all the pain. All of it. Do you hear me? I...repent... it... all!"

He screamed the words inside his skull. Again. To his own surprise, he found he meant them, truly. He waited, and...

Nothing happened.

Dust motes danced randomly in a shaft of sunlight. The skull, inverted, rocked, slowed, and was still.

The mind within remained sane, and aware.

And undying.

JAY ELSE

Epiphany

Eli limped into the outskirts of another small town. The first thing to do was to get some water, before he was thrown out of the place. He could survive another day without food, he thought, tightening the rope tied around his waist. He'd done it before now and probably would have to again. But water was a different matter.

He paused, trying to ease the fit of his sandal where it was rubbing the broken blister, and squinted up at the bright sun in the clear blue sky. The blood was sticky on his fingers, and he rubbed them against his worn jeans. He felt light-headed. Perhaps it was the sun. Perhaps it was the lack of food. But he knew it was neither of these; he felt a sense of foreboding and knew his light-headedness for a sign that God wanted him to prophesy again.

He glanced at the horizon, and saw the storm clouds gathering there. The same glance took in a few bare-footed children, sitting on the step of one of the old, stone buildings on either side of the road. The building looked abandoned, the front door hanging off its hinges, and no glass in the windows.

He shrugged his shoulders to settle his pack more comfortably – not that it was heavy, but it chafed against his bony shoulders – and continued on towards the town centre, where there would be a well, or a fountain, for him to drink from. He would also fill his water flask. He set off, stepping carefully, trying to avoid rubbing the blister. Maybe he should try and get a bandage or something.

He sensed, rather than heard, one of the children moving, and felt a thump in the middle of his back. He stumbled, but didn't turn. One of them had thrown a stone. The boy, he was bound to be the leader, was only doing it to impress the girl. If he turned, if he made eye-contact, the whole group would be on him. He shuffled along his way, not looking back. He could hear the girl's voice, scornful, but he could not make out the words.

It didn't matter. The foreboding had grown. He knew that not only would he speak the words of the Lord, but the people would reject them, and the Lord God would visit Death and Destruction on this place. The boy would suffer the vengeance of the Lord along with the rest of the town.

In the centre of the town, as he expected, there was a dusty square, with little eddies of straw and dust as the wind gusted, looking for a way out. A young girl – woman, he corrected himself – was winding a bucket up from a well. A small donkey, with a large number of flasks attached to straps, stood beside her.

It looked like this place didn't even have a fountain. He shuffled over towards her, ready to wait patiently for his turn to get some water.

She turned stiffly, as she heard him approach, then relaxed as she took in his gaunt appearance. He could see her thinking to herself "harmless." He felt his cheeks warm with embarrassment, and was thankful that with his tanned and weather-beaten face, it wouldn't show. No doubt she thought him older and weaker than he was, in his half-starved, dirty and bedraggled state. Anyone might recognise him for a prophet, he thought, but few would guess at the temporal authority he had once wielded.

Her look changed to pity, as he came up to the well, and she offered him a cup.

"Here, old man, drink this," she said.

It was milk. He raised it to his lips and tasted it. Cows' milk. Slightly soured. Perhaps two days old, maybe only one day in this heat. Where was the cow? It was hard to imagine that anyone could keep a cow here. His stomach rumbled with hunger and he drank in gulps. Perhaps she had walked into town from elsewhere, for a pure water supply. The milk must have been for her own midday meal; it must be her own cup. He wondered what diseases she had. It didn't matter – she had survived the plagues as had he, and if he hadn't suffered from anything long before this, he was immune. Besides, God would protect him for His purpose.

"Thank you, child," he said, "will you accept my blessing?" She didn't deserve to die with all the rest, he thought. Like Lot and Lot's wife, fleeing from Sodom and Gomorrah, she should have a chance to escape the destruction that would come.

Her look was still pitying, but she came to a decision. "Yes, I'll accept a blessing," she said.

He knew she thought she was humouring a madman. Perhaps her thought was more generous, to humour an old man merely addled by misfortune. "But I'm not old," he wanted to say.

He swung the pack around in front of himself, and reached inside. "Holy ointment," he explained. This was risky, but she deserved to be saved.

She said nothing, but waited, without expression, without curiosity.

He dipped his thumb into the ointment, and quickly, before she could dodge, he marked a sign on her forehead.

She frowned in annoyance, and wiped her head with the back of her hand, smearing the ointment onto the thin skin there. She looked as if she were about to say something, but then rubbed her hand, sighed and said, "You should've warned me what you were going to do."

Eli was relieved. The ointment looked liked vaseline – petroleum jelly – and was almost odourless, just like vaseline. In fact, more than ninety-nine percent it *was* vaseline. But she could have reacted more angrily.

Even so, it was time to leave her. He was almost immune to the ointment, although he still found it made him more relaxed. Eli smiled apologetically.

"Thank you again," he said, and shuffled over to sit in the shade at one side of the square.

She frowned at him again, shrugged, and went back to filling water flasks. He waited for the ointment to take effect. It was absorbed through skin. She would start to be saved in less than half an hour. And he hadn't prophesied.

Eli awoke with a start. Someone had kicked him in the ribs. Not hard, just enough to wake him. The shadows of several other men fell across his body, as he struggled to sit up.

"Move along," the man said, "we don't allow vagrants to hang around the square."

Eli, blinked, with the setting sun in his eyes. Off to one side, he could see another gang of children had gathered. Or perhaps it was the same gang. They wouldn't make trouble while the men were watching, but they could be a problem later, if he couldn't find somewhere safe to sleep.

First he needed to eat. He would feel better for some bread and soup, or whatever he could get here.

"Need some food," he croaked, his mouth dry, but tasting bad from sour milk and hunger.

The man pointed towards one of the roads leading off from the square. Eli turned and began shuffling in the direction the man had pointed out. One of the other men tripped him, and he fell, bruising his arm. He heard some of the children snigger.

The man who had tripped him now kicked him in the backside. "That's all the food you're going to get," he said.

Their leader stopped the kicker. "Let him be," he said, and to Eli, "just get out of our town. We don't want your kind of trash here."

Eli was suddenly angry. He stood up, filled with the righteous anger of a prophet of God. He faced the men, and saw the familiar flashing lights that always presaged the presence of the Lord. He was going to prophesy after all.

Facing the men, and the children, they seemed to glow with black halos, and the sky seemed darkened, even though he could still see clearly. Surely the Lord was with him.

He spoke, chastising them for their wickedness, their lack of charity to strangers, and he was filled with the Spirit of the Lord. They laughed as he warned them of vengeance if they did not mend their ways, and when his words moved them to anger, he smote the evil-doer who had tripped him.

When he woke again, he found they had dumped his unconscious body outside the town. His pack was still strapped to his back. He dimly remembered the beating, the kicking, and the children spitting at him. It hurt when he breathed, but he did not think any ribs were broken. It was difficult to be sure.

It was dark, perhaps after midnight; he was chilled to the bone, with the blinding headache that always came after he had prophesied. He would have to risk a trip back to the town square for water, and also because this town did indeed deserve the vengeance of the Lord.

He made his way quietly, and even more slowly than the first time, to the square at the centre of the town. All was quiet. He drank quietly with cupped hands from the bucket, remembering to fill his water flask, and then he washed his face, wincing at the cuts and bruises.

Now it was time to summon the Lord's vengeance. He reached into his pack, and brought out the postage-stamp sized homing beacon. He activated it, and wedged it into a crack in the low wall around the well. Now he was ready to leave, and he set off as fast as he could. He needed to be at least two miles clear, and behind cover, before the tactical nuclear warhead descended from orbit in an hour's time.

Following the trail of old, dried donkey droppings, he came to a well-tended house on the outskirts of the town. This must be where the girl who had shown him kindness lived. He found her lying in the mud outside the front gate of the house.

There was no sign of the donkey. It was not clear if the neuro-toxin in the vaseline, a "humane" chemical warfare agent, had affected her before or after she had got home. In any case, there was unlikely to be any other explanation for why she was lying asleep in a mud-puddle in the middle of the night.

She awoke still dazed as he took her hand, and pulled her to her feet. The Lord had prophesied through him truly, again – she would be saved, provided he could lead her to safety behind the hill within the next forty minutes. Otherwise, he mused, they both would join her neighbours as pillars of salt, although pillars of ash would be more accurate.

He wondered how she would thank him, when the effects of the drug wore off.

OLIVER ANDREW

Family Tree

A death in the family: someone must stop the rot.
So I sit baffled by these printed blanks.
How to unravel frustrations, thanks,
Memories, goodwill, petty deceit?
Strip them to consanguinity
Marriage and filiality,
A breastbone scoured fleshless, pure moonlit coral.

A roaring slope of water
Nags away at this island;
The alders are cut off, are undermined,
Topple; only a few dour resisters
Hang on longer. But something there must be
This universal falling can't fall through -
Recording what I know is true:
Dates, places, he or she.

And surely it's the wrong way up?
No tree from air closes into buds,
Branches, wood, cambium, then thuds
To ground and takes grip.
Turn it round? But now what root
In thick-laced darkness plaits a tree,
Lobbing a ponderous me
Into the future, and takes flight?

What am I? a meeting-place
For branches and roots?
A disentangler of disputes?
A safety-net? a slice?
A black hole threaded on DNA?
What am I doing here in mid-air,
Sole link of past and future? will a prayer
Fading in not-yet-born minds be me?

And then what tree?
Pregnant magnolia? or durable oak?
A tangly mangrove would be more like
(and would better suit me) -
Aerial roots, close collateral plants -
Some bits, though, don't go anywhere,
Failing to soar or disappear:
Dead leaves, tinder, aunts.

Patterns here weren't there in life,
Those individuals, whose grainy prints
Made them known at once,
Had enough with their own grief,
Memories, mistakes, quarrels, doubt,
To make their lives make sense
And not black fossils in a moonlit trance;
No wonder they kept some well blanked-out -
                    Let them go.

Funerals

They had real funerals then; the black-plumed horse,
Black-velvet-draped doorways, a book to sign;
Clutches of wailing women behind the hearse
Led through the streets to the churchyard, where
We stood for hours bare-headed in the rain,
Listening to our voices seal the dead in.

Now all's uncertain: we find something to wear,
Though dark of course; drive up separately; stand
Staring at nothing; a friend says something brief,
Praying's unfamiliar; women and children sniff;
But the men are still like moorland -
Steady, formidable, expressionless.
What's hidden here? Don't men feel grief?
Can't I cry too? Why do our mothers teach us this?

Lines on the beach

light light blue

fuzzy grey

a dark blue flecked with white

as is the turquoise, calming

to ochre-brown shallows

pale wavering children

off-white sand

a rainbow of parasols and sunbeds

those between tan and pink

these between me and you

Mirror

Excavating a dug-out on the Somme,
I find a soldier under the red clay.
There's a mirror in his hand still;
He must have been combing his hair
As that shell cRRRumped ninety years ago
With a scream that's left him open-mouthed.
Meticulously I disentangle it
From loosened phalanges and metacarpals,
To bag it with his buttons, combs and badges.
I certainly don't look in.

Pelican

This clownish pterodactyl
        wide-mouthed, smug, chin in,
banks heavily up, then
opening out umbrella-like
 but raggedy cruciform
 folds, as it falls, to an arrowhead.
        Stab!

Beautiful after all.

Safety First

Smoking kills.
Pork's forbidden. And beef.
Liver, raw eggs, unpasteurised milk - better not.

And keep away from salt,
Sugar, hydrogenated fats and oils,
Coffee, gluten, nuts; alcohol of course.

As for nitrates, pesticides, antibiotics,
GM foods, try to stay calm but who knows?

Luckily stress is good for you.

Looking right back

Not really sensitive, nor the stuff of dreams,
Some friends who turned to enemies and back,
OK at lessons, not so good at games.
I felt sorry for the poor in the abstract
But scared of scummies in their concrete estate.
A few parental snubs, mostly deserved;
Later, in turn, a monk, a mind, a mate,
To be rejected by a girl who laughed.

Nothing special - that was as far as it went.
Is this what shaped me? made me what I am?
None of that famishing? that disappointment?
No "seminal epiphanies"? no blighting shame?
No gold returns from guilt-edged investment?

And whether there was or not, now seems the same.

Memory

I had my fortune told in Moscow once,
In Space-and-Technology Park or somewhere.
An over-looked gipsy emerged from the bushes,
Bare-foot baby on hip, right hand outstretched,
Though access to the future was nationalised.
Amused, subversive, unthreatened, I complied.
Some hocus-pocus with the cupro-nickel -
She said I'd marry and have two children,
    Well, that was a tricky one!
Only then realised I wasn't Russian;
Fact-filled locals, starved of magic, might believe,
But superstitious foreigners......? She fled.

In case you're wondering, yes, she was right: she guessed
Where I was going. But not how I came to be.
Real magic is in access to the past;
We may survive thanks to forgetfulness,
But understanding's born in memory.

Choice

Erosion clarifies,
The future's no time for disguise.

Somewhere now, like Sinbad,
I'm carrying a crotchety, self-centred,

Aggressively boring, opinionated,
Garrulous, grumpy, grey-beard.

Or do I get a choice?
Couldn't I simply rejoice?

Watch the silty current pass?
Smile with the grandchildren on the grass?

Accept the clear night?
Give up the fight?

NATALIE CURTIS

Daddy

Just sitting by the window. Staring out. I know you can only come from one direction but like in any movie, where logic doesn't count, I look both ways. A car comes past every minute or so, with enough space in between so you can actually hear their engines coming down the road. Each time that noise resounds through the paper-house walls I leap off the sofa and press my nose to the grime. My face looks like it's been pressed into the dead ground outside, by now. I haven't looked at the clock. I don't want to see how late you are. This way, the time is only passing in my head.

Another rumble, another leap, another millimetre of dirt added to the collection on the tip of my nose. Your nose, or so I'm told. At least recently. There's a break in the traffic. I wait for another rumble, the engine grinding within the case, the tyres crunching on the asphalt. The only noise is the void ringing in my ears. Silent white noise. And the slow ticking of the clock that I can't bring myself to look at. The scrap of paper in my hand is the only clue to you. I unfold it, minding the tears that run through it, this mangled scrap that has seen the palm of my hand, the space under my pillow, the hollow of my jewellery box. It feels so smooth under my fingers, worn to its fibres. These few numbers, fainter now than ever, I punch into the keypad and wait, my finger poised over the screen so I cannot see the hour. I wait, the ringing droning into my head. Ring. Ring. R- a click and a sob. One I hear. One, I can only assume that you do, as what I can only assume is your voice rings out.

Acceptance

I feel - lighter. It's gone, like kicking a habit, a monkey off your back, it's gone and now I feel lighter. I can get back to the original plan. Plans. Nothing in the way anymore, no brewing disruption, nothing to stop me carrying on how I please - my vices can continue unabashed, because that is the way I like them. There's no guilt. None. It's not like I was attached in any psychological sense of the word. It was something to be dealt with, and like the strong independent, forward-minded woman I am certain that I am, I dealt with it. There was no middle ground, my options were extreme and this is the one that, physically, is less likely to come back to haunt me. Cigarette. Oh, oh... Better than ever.

I'm not guilty. I didn't do anything wrong. You can't... You can't work, and travel, and meet people when you're tired and tied down and stuck with something like that. Because it's not just a few months of discomfort, chamomile for wine, folic acid for sleepers, lounging on the fucking sofa while the men start ignoring and the women start knitting - it's not just that. It's the aftermath. I'm not giving it up, giving it *all* up, what I worked for and tried for and made myself sick for, not for this thing that just appears like a burglar in the night and just steals it *all* away. It deserved to go - this whole affair has set me back a week at least, already.

And it's not like I won't ever give it up - the work thing. At some point, yes - I'll settle down and resign myself to the sofa and the supportive hand-pats and the inability to paint my toe-nails. Make a replacement. But just not *now*. Later, I'll do it - I'll make up for it when I'm good and ready. Work now. Life later.

Because, you know, it's not easy. It's not easy trying to be a fucking superman and a woman at the same time. Things are expected of you, from both camps. There's a code. A set of rules, traditions, that you're supposed to follow. And those rules - they're mutually exclusive. I just... I just figured I could do one and then the other. And just a few weeks ago, I was doing fine on my own, following my plan. If there was a book, a guide, a mentor, then maybe it would be easier, but... who the fuck can I talk to? The family camp – "Why are you wearing yourself out with all that work? You know what you need - you need to settle yourself down with a family." And, on the other, equally un-fucking-helpful hand, the work camp – "It's all about the job." Christ... At least... Fuck. At least before, this morning, there was someone there listening.

Summer Holiday

"Are you OK?"

Am I OK? I have little or no idea. As far as I can tell I'm still upright and my arms and legs are dancing, only not to anything like the beat of the poorly selected playlist. The fact that I'm not touching anyone in this miniature disco is stark enough to let a brain even this addled work out that people are giving me a wide berth. The more I try to work out whether or not I am indeed OK, the more the colours blend and swim and the face now peering intently into mine looks like it's being reflected off the back of a spoon. The faces in the crowd seep into the corners of my eyes and whilst focusing on them makes my stomach twist, I feel that they know something, see something, that I do not.

A hand slithers down my shoulders to my back and props me up, and I can only conclude that no, I am not OK.

Where am I where am I where am I? There that's my street oh no it fucking isn't why has he left me on my own on the side of the road what did I do why do I feel like this I've never felt like this before oh my god it was the drink the free drink oh holy jesus I've been spiked did they touch me did they get me by myself why did she leave me on my own it was supposed to be a girls' night is that my street no it's not oh my God on my own in the middle of the night in South America anything could happen those girls got raped here a few nights ago and now it's going to be me oh how could he leave me here by myself I told him the address I know I told him the fucking address... what's the fucking address what's the fucking address where the fuck do I live where am I where am I where am I?

A firm hand presses me down into a sodden chair and I find myself at the wrong end of the bar, next to the grimy barman and his grimier friend. I can't make out much but it's hard to ignore their smirking faces, grinning at the silly little English girl whose eyes are too big for her liver. Serpentine fingers are on my shoulder; their clammy touch and accompanying, overpowering wave of cheap aftershave conspire to my sickness. I can feel the rum rising in my throat and can barely keep it down enough to refuse the drink being thrust dizzyingly under my nose. A haze of foreign accent and the tinny echo of the latest tourist-driven track and that cup is still there, too close for comfort and smelling of knock-off Calvin Klein. I can't work out what language he's speaking, let alone what he's saying, but I'm suddenly oh-so-thirsty and wrap my limp, trembling hand around the plastic. The warm, flat mixture slides down my throat and I feel sick to my stomach again. I assumed it was a coke but the heat in my gut gives me other ideas. His slimy partner in crime is still watching me and I have to lean my elbows on the bar, head hanging down, breathe deeply just to stay awake.

Where am I where am I where am I? There that's my street oh no it fucking isn't where's my phone why didn't I bring my phone the one fucking night I should have brought it with me my first night on my own without the boys to keep an eye and no fucking battery can't even ring home where is home I don't even know where I am this isn't my street why didn't he bring me to my street I told him to stop why didn't he stop never do here what you wouldn't do at home and here I am wandering the streets at what time even is it it's still so dark where is everyone why is there no-one to help me what do I look like stop crying stop crying that isn't going to help is that yes I think it's a petrol station oh but everything's so fuzzy is that a taxi in front oh please help me I just want to go home.

The stench of smoke overloads my nostrils as a hand reaches through the crook in my arm and lifts my chin up and away from the sticky, slippery bar. Tobacco-stained teeth and a used car-salesman's smile hover into view and I squint, trying to put the colours inside the lines. The scene looks like it's been lifted from a child's painting book; watery, smudged, careless. The hand rests on my cheek and for a few, brief moments I am thankful for its support. The face looms towards my own and I feel hot breath in my ear, against my cheek, on my lips. Cigarettes and sin and the taste makes me want to gag but the fingers dig deep into my jaw and hold me still. I can't pull back; I can barely hold my own weight and my body feels heavier by the second. He won't let me go, and I have no choice, his carnal instincts are in charge now. I don't even wonder why no-one is coming to rescue me; I'm too weak to play the damsel in distress so when he lets go of my face and takes my hand instead, there's little I can do but let him lead me where he chooses.

Where am I where am I where am I? That's my street oh yes it fucking is and here we are oh thank you so much what the hell is John going to say where are my keys what the hell sort of state am I in stop crying you look like a fucking moron if he asks me what happened what do I say I don't even know myself I don't know where I've been what time is it now what time did I leave how did I get in that first fucking taxi and why didn't he bring me home oh no here we go I'm sorry I'm sorry I don't know I'm sorry I ran out of battery I'm sorry please stop shouting I don't know I'm sorry I need the bathroom I'll be right back we'll talk I'll try to remember but just let me go to the bathroom OK OK I'll be right back just stay there what the hell happened why am I so sore?

THE NIGHTWRITERS

Oliver Andrew worked for 27 years in a local sixth-form college. Now retired, Oliver has recycled himself as a French mountain peasant in the summer, returning to Brighton in the winter to keep warm. He would like to write novels and drama but can't, so sticks to poetry and non-fiction (travel, philately, history).

Noreen Brown has been a social worker and a dairy farmer in New Zealand and Australia, tramping round in wellies and helping her son-in-law on his rounds as a veterinarian. One of her fondest memories is driving a Combie in NZ to a rave. A long way from children all over the world, Noreen now potters (and writes) in her oh-so-respectable semi on the edge of Brighton.

Adrian Caines is a thirty something living in Brighton. He works for the city council as a social worker, working with adults with a learning disability.

Sean Campbell was formed in Coventry then sent to Brighton with a slight detour via York. Sean is currently working on a novel.

Colin Chalmers was born in Glasgow and now lives in Brighton. He has written for a number of publications including *Scottish Child*, *SchNEWS* and *The Big Issue* and is currently working on a novel.

Jonathan Chamberlain was brought up in Hongkong and Ireland. He has written a number of books including *Cancer: The Complete Recovery Guide* (www.fightingcancer.com). He is currently director of The Big Story Festival (www.bigstoryfestival.co.uk).

Natalie Curtis is an English and Languages student at Sussex University. In her spare time she enjoys red wine, cigarettes and not talking to other students.

Alasdair Craig is a 24 year old craftsman and award winning goldsmith. His recently found passion for books has inspired him to try to become a writer.

Simon Davis is a Brighton-based Welshman, husband of one and father of two.

Jay Else is the pen-name of Jonathan Cunningham. He was born in Brighton, went away, came back again and is still here.

Sian Evans joined Nightwriters after the sad demise of the Brunswick Poetry Society. Sian is a painter and sculptor as well as a writer - her sculptures are currently on display in Brighton's Tallula's Tea Rooms in memory of her last lover Stuart Slade who was murdered opposite the tea rooms in 2008. Sian is soon to lecture at Kashmir University on whether spriritualism exists within post-modernism.

Dennis Hickson was born in Croydon and spent three years living and travelling in Asia before moving to Brighton in 1995 where he completed an English degree and co-wrote a play that was performed at Concorde 2. He is interested in humour and tackling psychological and controversial subjects.

Liz Jalla started writing novels when she settled with her family in Brighton 30 years ago. Liz has recently finished her third novel *The Cherry Tree* and is preparing her first novel *A Feeling for Crows* for publication.

Lorna Kent was born in London, moved to Brighton to study illustration and liked it so much she stayed. Lorna writes for children as well as adults - she has written and illustrated six books for children and her poetry has twice won fifth place in the Cardiff Poetry Competition.

Enzo Marra is an artist and poet who has published in *Poetry Revolt, Unquiet Desperation, Rattlesnake Review, The Delinquent, Birds on the Line, Read This Magazine* and *Concrete Meat Sheet*. His artworks are represented by the Wilson Williams gallery in Hackney.

Alanna McIntyre loves the sounds of words, enjoys creative art and finds it therapeutic. Telling stories incorporating all the senses is a skill Alanna is developing and uses when working with children with special needs.

Tanya Murray used to do a lot in another life. Now she's trying really, really hard just to be.

Rob Paraman has been a Nightwriter for seven years and has almost finished his first novel, about teenagers growing up in Australia in 1977. His favorite writers are J.Krishnamurti and Katherine Mansfield.

Moss Rich started writing poems in 1975. He gets his ideas from the exploits of people he meets and from situations he finds himself in. Moss has published two books of poems and is at work on a third, which he hopes to see in print before climate change.

Tim Shelton-Jones has stopped work recently (as a computer analyst-programmer) but finds that more time somehow means less. Tim is still deeply involved in Nightwriters after many years though, and is still loving it.

Lightning Source UK Ltd.
Milton Keynes UK
30 January 2010